Also by Risqué

The Sweetest Taboo

RED LIGHT SPECIAL

One World | Ballantine Books | *New York*

Risqué

RED LIGHT SPECIAL

a novel

A One World Books Trade Paperback Original

Copyright © 2008 by Risqué

Published in the United States by One World Books, an imprint of The Random House Publishing Group, a division of Random House, Inc., New York.

ONE WORLD is a registered trademark and the One World colophon is a trademark of Random House, Inc.

LIBRARY OF CONGRESS CATALOGING-IN-PUBLICATION DATA
Risqué.
Red light special : a novel / Risqué.
p. cm.
ISBN 978-0-345-50431-9
1. Prostitutes—Fiction. 2. Police—Fiction. 3. Escort services—Fiction. 4. Undercover operations—New York (State)—New York—Fiction. 5. Manhattan (New York, N.Y.)—Fiction.
I. Title.
PS3618.I736R43 2008
813'.6—dc22   2008027397

Printed in the United States of America

www.oneworldbooks.net

2 4 6 8 9 7 5 3 1

Book Design by Laurie Jewell

*To Melody Guy, for your patience
and undying faith in my ability.
And to Nakea Murray, for always
knowing that this was possible.*

*To Danielle Santiago, Dywane Birch,
and Adrienne Byrd for the late nights and
early mornings, the five-hour shots,
and for always answering my calls when
I was pulling my hair out.*

ACKNOWLEDGMENTS

Lord, please grant me the courage to change the things that I can and the wisdom to know the difference. . . .

To my Father and Savior, Jesus Christ. There have been many times when I've thought about the day I prayed while sitting at a red light and asked You to bless me with a chance . . . never imagining that all of this would unfold. I thank You, Father, for Your grace, Your mercy, and Your favor.

To my mom and dad, I thank you for your support with my writing, but more than that, I thank you for loving my children, picking them up from school, dance class, and for simply being there.

To my Grandma (in that tiny town of Murfreesboro, North Carolina—with the three traffic lights and one yield sign), who swears I don't call or come see her enough. I promise you, I will call more often and stop asking you, "What in the world is there to do down there?" I love you, even though you keep calling me Sa'Sanda—LOL.

To my husband, who has always been my biggest supporter. Thank you for your patience, love, and understanding. My sweeties: Taylor, Sydney, and Zion, I love you soooooo much! I want so much to hand deliver you the world: I hope to teach you that dreams have no limits.

To my family, church family, and friends, your support is priceless and I hope to make you proud.

To my One World/Ballantine family, those seen and unseen, thank you so much for all that you do, I may have written the manuscript but together we made this a book.

To Adrienne Byrd and Ms. Dennesha Diamond, I thank you so much for talking to me three, four, five times a day, staying up with me sometimes from 9:00 P.M. until 6:00 in the morning as I wrote this story. You are a brilliant author and I speak nothing but wonderful things about you.

To Danielle Santiago, who insisted that I stop what I was doing and read about the infamous scandal. You are a wonderful author with a world of potential! So climb over the rocks and continue on your road to greatness.

To Dywane Birch, you are such a gem and I'm so glad that we're friends. I get so inspired when I speak to you, because I see what positive thinking and believing in one's ability can do.

Nakea, Nakea, Nakea, all I have to say is that where would Risqué be if you hadn't told me: "Stop it right now—Risqué doesn't go to church!" LOL! I love you so much, my friend, you are an unselfish inspiration and I can't wait for the day when I pick up "On Air."

To K'wan, you are a brilliant author and a wonderful friend. Thanks a million for talking to me when I was stressed out and needed advice on how to write crazy shi*t! (LOL).

Keisha, I guess we've both learned that the book world is certainly a venture. Always remember to be true to yourself, that God is the only One in control, and never forget who your true friends are.

Anna J and Erik Gray, much success to you!

To my coworkers, you all have been some of my greatest supporters! Thanks could never be enough, and to my unit: Remember, we're down like four flats!

To the bookstore, message boards, vendors, reviewers, and book clubs, thanks so much for your support in all of my literary ventures.

And saving the best for last, the fans. I have the best fans in the world! You all have opened your arms and embraced all of my literary works. You e-mail me and ask me questions, and I enjoy hearing from you. You all have helped to make this possible. Thank you so much! I would love to hear from you again, so be sure to e-mail me at Risque215@aol.com

Also, be sure to listen to me and my crew—Nakea Murray and Tiffany Colvin (hey, Tiffany!) every Wednesday night at seven on blogtalk radio, "Three Chicks On Lit."

Oh, and remember, this is fiction, so do not try this at home and if you do, then use a condom! Now let's turn the page and do the damn thing! (And in the great words of Erykah Badu— "I'm an artist and I'm sensitive about my sh*t. So be easy."— LOL!)

Love ya,
Risqué

KILLAH PUSSY

ONE

Four A.M.

Her eyes scanned the high-rise loft, drifting from the black satin sheets on the unmade bed to the strips of moonlight on the hardwood floor.

She sat crouched in the corner, knees folded into her chest, as she ran her hands through loose strands of hair that framed her face. Ashes from her cigarette fell between her knees as the faint sound of music drifted in from the apartment next door.

The octagon creases of the Crown Royal bottle reflected her disheveled appearance as a silenced and loaded 9 millimeter pistol lay next to her bare feet. She wiped the snot dripping from her nose, rose from the floor, and slipped her kitten heel mules on. Her head pounded with a migraine as she thought of all the fucked-up choices he made.

How he never once thought about her and about all the nights she cried. She wondered why he was doing this, why her love wasn't enough. She'd already accepted that she wasn't number one, but now she had to come behind a thousand-dollar-a-night-trick-ho.

She looked at the clock. Five A.M.

As her heels clicked, sounding out an offbeat rhythm across the hardwood floor, she heard keys jingling in the front door. She panicked. She didn't want him to know she was here . . . at least not yet. She wanted to expose him, but not like this. She knew she didn't have enough time to make it to the back door, so she ran into the hallway coat closet and retreated into the darkened corner, careful not to make any noise.

A few paranoia-filled seconds later, she eased closer to the door's plantation louvers. From there she could see into the bedroom.

The smell of the cologne she'd given to him for his birthday drifted into the hallway, along with another, softer scent, confirming that he was not alone.

The couple came in from the dimly lit hallway, practically tripping over each other, their kissing silhouette reflected on the floor. She could see him biting the woman's bottom lip. She yanked his shirt open, the buttons spilling onto the floor like spare change.

As they moved closer to the balcony and moonlight shone on the bitch's face, she realized she'd seen her before. Eve was her name, and she was his regular whore.

The private eye she'd hired had told her that although there were others, Eve was his bottom bitch.

She watched him pick up the remote to the stereo, and moments later WBLS' *Quiet Storm* filled the air.

"Eve," he said, breathing heavily, "come over here, baby." He sat down in a red leather chair and Eve straddled him, rubbing the dripping silk from her wet pussy across his welcoming shaft.

"What you want, daddy?" She bit the side of his neck and gyrated her hips, her skirt easing over her naked ass.

He gripped both sides of her luscious behind and pressed his fingers deeply into her cheeks. "Get up and turn around." Once her back was facing him, he ran his middle finger up her slit and then licked it.

Eve moaned. "Daddy, suck it . . ."

"Say please." He twirled his finger in and out, moving from her ass to her wetness, back and forth and back again.

"Oh, daddy, please . . . ," Eve pleaded, feeling her pussy drip. "Please."

He raised her dress completely over her apple ass and pulled her closer. Her behind was so beautiful that he stopped for a moment to kiss it. Then he took his tongue, opened her wetness, and licked it. He licked it hard at first and then soft, as if he wanted to prolong the moment.

"Harder, daddy," she pleaded.

He lapped his tongue up and down while he slapped both of her cheeks.

"Harder!" she lustfully demanded.

Without hesitation he stuck his tongue directly into her. Eve screamed, and her knees became weak, causing her to tilt forward. He hooked his arm around her waist and pulled her back so she wouldn't fall. Taking his left hand and playing in her creamy canal, he said, "I should make you pay me for this shit." He slapped one of her ass cheeks and bit the other. As he stuck three fingers into her pussy she began to do a Jamaican wine on his fingertips, her luscious moneymaker kissing his lips with every movement of her hips.

"Oh, daddy," Eve said as his teeth sank into the meat of her ass, her pussy salivating from every ounce of sweet pain.

"Shake your ass in my face," he insisted.

Eve did as he instructed, and he slapped her on the ass again. "I want more! Shake it in my face harder!"

She threw her hips in motion, causing her cheeks to groove like jelly.

"Motherfucker," he said through gritted teeth, "what the fuck I tell you to do? You fuckin' playing with me?"

"Na-na-na-nooooo . . . !" she stuttered. "I would never do that."

"You better not." He placed his hands on both of her hips and shook them, causing her bottom to jiggle wildly.

Eve could tell by the way he spoke that he was due to cum at any moment, so she spread her ass cheeks and his face disappeared in between. "Suck it! Oh my Gawd, please suck it . . ." It felt so good that for a moment Eve couldn't remember what language she spoke: Spanish, English, Haitian patois . . . something . . . anything to help her understand how she was able to scream in a falsetto.

As he continued to lap the creamy pinkness of her sweetness, he panted and slid to his knees. Eve started working her clit over his tongue. She could feel her orgasm stirring intensely in her belly. Eve knew at any moment she was due to see the heavens and the stars and travel to a place far beyond space. Eve bit into her bottom lip as she closed her eyes. The sound of him tugging on her pussy lips filled the room.

He held her hands as he lay flat on his back and seduced Eve to spread her love over his face. Her chest heaved as tears blinded her eyes and within an instant she came twice. Afterward he picked her up, roughly slid her dress off, walked her out of the bedroom and over to the kitchen sink, and sat her on top. He reached behind her to turn the hot water on and let the steam rise between her legs.

The woman in the closet shifted to peer out through the slightly open door.

"When I throw this dick at you," he said in a lustful rage, "you better throw it back or this hot water gon' scald that ass."

"Wait," Eve said, feeling a spray of the steamy water popping against her skin. "That's enough role play." She pushed him slightly. "You being a little too freaky."

"Oh, you denying me?" he said as he slid his nine and a half inches of crooked dick into her cum-filled slit. "You gon' take this dick."

She gasped. "Okay, okay," she gasped again. "But take the stopper out the sink."

"Hell no!" He thrust into her with all his might. "Now throw it back!"

Bracing her hands against the sides of the sink, she returned his stroke and ended up knocking over the plates in the dish rack, sending them crashing to the floor. There was some Crown Royal on the concrete countertop, and it too toppled over, with some of it running into the sink and the rest spilling onto the floor.

Eve arched her back as high as she could, giving him full access to her melting sugah walls.

The music from his dick seeped into the closet as the woman inside studied the motion of his balls banging between Eve's thighs. The sound of their skin slapping burned her ears.

He gripped the edge of the windowsill behind the sink, breathed heavily into Eve's ear, and pounded into her as if his life depended on it.

Judging by the way her body jerked, Eve knew her back had

to be broken, but she did her best to quickly recuperate, as his strokes came in forceful succession. Eve tossed and turned and squirmed, dipping a portion of her ass into the scalding water rising behind her. She wanted desperately to tell him to stop the water and to let her go, but the mixture of pain, pleasure, and the unknown caused her to cum from the top of her head to the bottom of her feet. All she could do was lay her head on the windowsill and struggle to breathe.

"What the fuck you all quiet for?" he said as he pounded into her.

"I'm tryna figure out," she managed to squeak out, "why you got such a big dick if you ain't workin' it."

Holding her waist and grinding into her, he threw her left leg over his shoulder and wrapped the right one around his waist. "Oh, I ain't workin' this dick?"

Just as Eve was about to say something slick, she couldn't hold it in any longer. "Jesus!" Her head started to spin and she felt as if she were traveling in a whirlwind: Paris, Rome, Milan, Puerto Rico, home, and back again. All she could see was sweet blackness as she clawed her nails down his back, drawing blood, and cum rushed like tidal waves between her thighs.

"You better not be cummin'," he instructed her. "Always fucking with me and shit." He bit her chocolate drop nipples, her full breasts feeling like silk against his lips.

The woman continued to watch from the closet, and as tears fell from her eyes, she looked at his face and knew what he was about to say. "You love this dick, baby?" he said as she mouthed the words along with him.

"I don't know," Eve spat. "You haven't given me a reason why I should love it yet."

He threw Eve a hard hip and yanked a fistful of her hair, causing her neck to jerk back. "You fucking with me?" He took her legs and folded them Indian style across her chest. "What, you can't take this big dick?"

"No," she struggled to say as he made her ass rise off the sink. "I'm just tryna figure out why you ain't workin' it." He pounded her, and a portion of her ass brushed the scalding water. "Ah!"

"I'm workin' it?"

"No."

He pounded her again, and this time the hot water felt more intense than before.

"Ah!" she screamed.

"You feel it?"

"No!" She squirmed, his dick pounding against her explosive G-spot.

He thrust into her again, and his dick felt as if it was expanding. "You feel it?"

She couldn't answer. Her mouth couldn't fix itself to form another lie.

"Answer me!"

With every thrust the hot water scalded her ass. Eve knew there had to be something wrong with getting turned on by the hot water, but the pain was no different from melted candle wax, a sensation she also enjoyed. She could feel her climax preparing to take flight and soak his dick. "I'm cummin', baby."

"Don't cum before you tell me you feel this dick!"

"I feel it!" she screamed. "Oh God, I feel it!"

His nut burst like a breaking dam through the tip of his dick. "Goddamn!" he said, releasing his cum into her as he held onto the windowsill behind her. "That was the shit." He kissed her lips.

Eve couldn't answer; all she could do was breathe.

"You love me, baby?" he said as his chest heaved.

"Yes, daddy." She could breathe a little easier now. "I do."
He looked at Eve. "I want you in my life . . . all the time."
A smile lit up her face, "Are you serious?"
"Yes."
"And the others?"
"Fuck them. They're over. You're the only woman for me.
No more denying you, no more of you being in the shadows.
I'm taking you away from all of the street corners, the pimps,
and the bullshit in your life and I'm making you mine. Fuck
everything else and everybody else. It's about you and me." He
kissed Eve on the lips again. "There's no other woman for me."

The woman in the closet fell against the wall. She didn't care
if they'd heard her or not. She didn't know whether to be in
shock or to not believe what she'd just seen. Something had to
be wrong. He wouldn't do this to her, he wouldn't. He couldn't
be this strung out that he would let retail pussy dictate his fate.

There was no way he would choose some other bitch after
all they'd been through. Certainly, he wouldn't take all that
she'd done, dismiss it, and then allow this bitch to reap the
benefits.

She looked into his face and hoped to see some type of con-
firmation that he loved her the way she loved him. Yet when
she saw the way he stared at Eve, his feelings were clear. He
regarded Eve with a gaze she'd never seen. Now she was certain that he was seriously trying to oust her so he could set up
shop with this streetwalking bitch.

Her life was over. There was nothing she could do to undo
this. He'd crossed the line, and somehow she needed to make
him pay for lying, cheating, and throwing her away as if she'd
been a shitty piece of tissue stuck to his shoe.

The sounds of them beginning to make love again invaded
her space, directing her anger to the bitch in there with her
man. As he passionately kissed and stroked Eve, she pointed

the gun in their direction, blasting it through the closet door. The hollow-point bullet soared through the wooden planks and within a millisecond of an instant invaded Eve's skull.

Oblivious, he stroked with his eyes closed against his now-still lover, while their invisible guest quietly opened the closet door and slid out of the apartment. A few moments later as she stepped on the elevator, WBLS' *Quiet Storm* and his screams created an operatic choir behind her.

TWO

Me'Shell NdegéOcello's *Plantation Lullabies* echoed in the background of Gracie Mansion's master suite as the blue lights shone from the face of the Bose surround-sound stereo that filled the historic bedroom with music.

Monday Smith lay naked in the center of her king-sized bed. She couldn't believe that here she was again, with a rotating and vibrating lipstick dildo in her hand, and contemplating masturbation, as if she didn't have a husband. As if she were actually some kind of lonely-ass pathetic freak and not married to the mayor of New York City.

From the outside looking in she was a gem: skin that glowed like Egyptian gold with hints of caramel in its richest form, melting milk chocolate eyes, thick size-twelve hips, and sexy African and perfectly shaped lips.

However, if anyone had paid any attention they would've seen that her husband, the recently re-elected Mayor Kenyatta Smith, wasn't shit and he used his charm, wit, power, and position to perfect being a shit. No matter how polished his veneer was in public, in private he was an arrogant, selfish, and ghetto-acting motherfucker.

He'd had numerous affairs, and no matter what Monday did, how beautiful, how successful, or how good at giving head she was, at the end of the night he crept into a world where his mistresses became his wife.

Monday spread her legs and parted her moist and dripping vulva. She massaged the chilling dildo over the hood of her hardening clit. Her body quivered with each vibrating stroke as she circled the dildo's tip over her clit, over her trembling lips, and then slid it between her slit and let it electrify her cherry.

As her orgasm stirred she massaged a wet fingertip over her nipples and thought about how she needed Kenyatta's raspy voice to whisper in her ear and his hot breath to land at the base of her neck. She needed him to treat her like she was someone he desired. However, as she lay on the bed amidst the fifteen-hundred–thread count Egyptian cotton sheets with a thrilling, yet unfulfilling, explosion between her thighs, all she had left was a nightly wet spot and a reoccurring thought of how much her husband lied.

"Damn it!" Monday sighed as tears gathered in her eyes. "This is ridiculous!"

She sat up, slid to the edge of the bed, crossed her legs, and reached for a cigarette. As she blew a stream of smoke toward the dark vaulted ceiling she wondered when she'd begun to settle for this kind of treatment. Exactly when did she start accepting Kenyatta's affairs and playing with herself as a part of their marriage? She wished she could call someone for advice, but whom would she call? No one outside of the political realm would understand that this was about much more than losing a marriage, being unappreciated, and being damaged emotionally. That was the easy shit; she could get therapy for that. But this . . . this was a whole other level of violated commitment that other people's mortgages, kids, bills, dogs, and shit couldn't even fuck wit'.

The average everyday heartbreak had nothing on this. Yeah, she loved her husband, but this . . . this was about upholding an image, maintaining power, prestige, and position. And Monday wasn't about to lose her life without a fight. She'd worked too hard, sacrificed too much, climbed too far.

Monday's heart danced in her chest as she stood in the middle of the carpeted floor, her eyes skipping around the room, wondering just how long he had been stringing her along.

They'd met ten years ago in law school. His smile had captivated her and the attraction was too obvious for either of them to dismiss, so they kicked it and soon found out they had everything in common, from listening to the same music and appreciating the same art to having traveled to the same places. They even had the same sense of humor. In three months they considered it fate and married in a small ceremony.

At first it was perfect. He had political aspirations and she had an unfulfilled yearning for recognition. So along with being in love with him, his rising career was just the mission she needed to become the wife of New York City's most prestigious politician.

She managed his campaigns and groomed him as he went from community board member to City Council member to state representative, until the day she suggested he run for mayor. He agreed and said he'd always wanted to run New York City, so they put their plan in motion. Monday made sure Kenyatta rubbed elbows only with those who could help him get to the next step. No more hanging out with anyone they couldn't network and politick with. She made sure he was at all the necessary rallies, supported just the right charities, fed the homeless, held AIDS babies, joined a church, shot basketball with the high school kids in the park, and dressed as Santa to deliver toys to poor children on Christmas. And when election time came, everyone not only knew Kenyatta's name but also felt they knew what he stood for and had a personal connection with him. He was a shoo-in.

Not long after he was elected to office their marriage began to change, and now here she sat in the cool of the predawn, trying to figure out what the fuck was really going on.

Tired of sulking, Monday showered, climbed back into bed, and drifted to sleep. Hours later she heard the bed creak.

"Monday."

It was Kenyatta. She felt his weight press down next to her while he tugged a little at the sheet pulled up over her breasts. "Monday, I need you to wake up." She could tell by the sound of his voice that something was wrong.

She stretched as she lifted her sleep mask off her face. She looked at the clock—7:00 A.M.—and then back at him. "Where have you been, Kenyatta?"

He shook his head, and a muscle in his jaw twitched, a sure sign that he was about to lie. If she knew him as well as she thought she did, he would start by saying he'd been out thinking.

"I've been up all night," he squinted, his honey-glazed face looking as if his mind were recalling a difficult memory, "thinking about some shit."

Monday sat up. The last time he'd spoken like this, there was a distressed mistress and an abortion they needed to make disappear. Monday looked at him and blinked. "And after you finish telling me what's on your mind," she said, stroking his cheek, "I want you to think of another lie to convince me that you weren't out fucking some bitch all night."

"Here we go—"

"Or would you rather I smell your dick?"

"This is why we can't talk." He hopped off the bed, the wrinkles in his lavender dress shirt swaying with his body as he paced the floor, doing his all to hide that he was a nervous wreck inside. "You're my wife, not some jump-off, and I'm trying to talk to you. Keep it real with you. I'm trying to drop the political mayoral talk right now and kick it like we used to."

"What?"

"You know I love you."

"Kenyatta, please. Just tell me, is it a new bitch or an old resurrected jawn."

"See?" He pointed at her. "See what you do? And then you wonder why I don't tell you anything, why we aren't best friends. It's because I can't confide in you anymore. I come to you and tell you that I've been up all night and you don't even care to know why? Instead you get all hyped and shit, and accuse me of some faceless chick? Fuck them bitches in the street. You're the only woman for me. And I know I haven't been perfect . . ." He paused, walked over to the bed, and kneeled on one knee. "And yeah," he said calmly, "I have some flaws, but I've tried to right my wrongs as best I could." Monday looked at the hand he'd rested on the bed and wondered why it was shaking.

Kenyatta rose from the floor and continued on. "I stayed up many nights trying to figure out what's best for the city, my family, and lastly for me. I place everyone's needs before mine and I'm okay with that, because putting others before me is just the type of man I am."

Monday stared at him, amazed he was giving a speech. She

knew that at any moment he would tell her she was all he needed.

"And you know you're all I've ever needed, and I need you now more than ever."

Monday's heart dropped as she folded her arms across her breasts. "Let me smell your dick, so I can get this over with. You're taking too long to get to the goddamn point, and I don't have time to talk! I wanna know where you've been, because in a minute"—she opened her nightstand drawer, pulled out her .22, and slammed it on the nightstand—"I'ma shoot a bitch!"

Instantly Kenyatta's mind flashed back to Eve's death and he wondered where Monday had been last night. He quickly looked around the room. Swallowing the memory of Eve's blood covering him, he walked over to the nightstand, picked up the gun, and checked the clip.

"What the fuck are you doing?" Monday asked.

"Just making sure you ain't lost your motherfuckin' mind last night!"

"Last night? What the hell happened last night?"

Ignoring her question and confirming that the gun hadn't been fired, he tossed it back into the drawer. "Where you go last night? You went out?"

"I know goddamn well—" Monday paused. "You ain't questioning me. I don't know what kinda beam-me-up-Scotty Jedi mind tricks you tryna pull negro, but I'm not the one. Now where yo' black ass been?"

"Why do you act so damn crazy? You are the mayor's wife!"

"Motherfuck being the mayor's wife. The mayor is the reason I'm going the fuck crazy!" She flung her arms in the air. "Now where have you been?"

Kenyatta stared at Monday and thought about how much she flipped. He knew if she didn't think twice about jumping on him and he made two of her, she wouldn't hesitate to kill a bitch, but then again . . . maybe not. He looked into her eyes and saw the hurt reflected in her glance. "I've just had some shit on my mind. There's a lot of pressure at the job right now, being mayor and being responsible for everybody in the city."

"What the fuck are you talking about? I didn't ask for your resumé! I don't wanna hear that. You've been gone since yesterday morning and you walk in here singing some 'I got too much on my mind' love song shit at seven o'clock the next morning and you think I'm going to sit here and buy it? Niggah, please. Fuck you think this is?"

"Goddamn, Monday, why can't you ever just believe anything that I say? You just stress me too much. That's why I do some of the things I do, because you push me to." He started pacing the room again.

Monday stared, taken aback. "What the—?" was all she could think to say. She swallowed. Now she knew for sure he was cheating. Because every time, every single time, he acted like this, she knew his feelings were torn because he was back to fucking with some sideline bitch. "Just tell me, which bitch is it this time? Taryn again?"

"Can it ever be what I tell you it is?"

"Donnica?"

"Do you always have to assume it's someone else?"

"Must be a new bitch!"

"You just never stop, Monday! Damn do you know how much I sacrifice for you?"

"Sacrifice?" Monday was completely floored. "Sacrifice? I'll tell you what to sacrifice, sacrifice some of them tricks you fuckin' wit! Sacrifice me always being home alone. Sacrifice that shit, Mr.-Fuckin'-Mayor!"

"Monday, you're selfish as hell! You know how badly I want a baby, but you refuse to get pregnant, and here I am still standing by you and you don't even acknowledge that!"

Monday blinked in disbelief. He knew she struggled with her weight. Being that he cheated all the time, she couldn't take the chance of becoming larger than a size twelve, and even that was too much. Which is how she ended up on a thousand diets. Atkins, Slim-Fast, Jenny Craig, hot dogs, eggs, cabbage, lemonade and cayenne pepper . . . she even tried the Subway diet, and at the end of the day all she ended up with was an abnormal thyroid and twenty extra pounds to contend with. "I don't believe you said that!"

"And I don't believe you keep questioning me. Do you know how you make me feel when you continue to accuse me of things?"

Monday blinked again. Every time they had an argument Kenyatta always twisted the shit around and made himself out to be the victim. "I'm sick of you always fucking up! And I have to deal with the consequences!"

"Step then, Monday! Since you so tired and nothing I do is good enough, then bounce. Catch yo' ass around. Shit, I'm tired of arguing about how much our marriage means to me. Fuck it. If you tired, then I'm the fuck exhausted!" He flicked his hand as if he'd just performed a magic trick and then he turned his back on her and headed out the room.

Feeling as if he'd just told her to kiss his ass, Monday flew off the bed, pulled her hand back, and slapped the shit out of him. And then without warning she threw her whole body on top of him, fighting him as if she were tussling for her life.

In an effort to get her off of him, he flung her across the room.

She hit a wall and fell to her ass before getting up and storming toward him again. Kenyatta grabbed Monday by the shoulders and shook her like a rag doll. "I need you to get yourself together!" he spat. "I'm trying to save my damn career, this marriage, and protect you—"

"Protect me?" Monday shouted. "How the fuck were you trying to protect me? A blind kindergartner coulda played Superman better than yo' whack ass! You tryna protect me? Am I being punk'd?" She moved her head from side to side. "Is this a fuckin' joke? "Why don't you tell me the truth for once," Monday seethed, "instead of all this nonsense? If you are going to cheat, then you oughta man up to it!" She waved her hand around the room. "You no-good, worthless piece of gutter rat shit! Unappreciative Uncle Tom motherfucker! I don't know who the hell voted you in office, yo' ass doesn't deserve to be the mayor of Mayberry let alone New York City! And the day you are out of office is the day motherfuckers can get a real politician in here!"

Kenyatta grabbed Monday by her neck and pushed her into the corner of the room. Her words cut through him. He squeezed the sides of her throat. "Who the fuck are you talking to?" He squinted at her, his veins thumping from the sides of his smooth bald head to his thick neck. "Why would you say some shit like that?"

"You need to learn to tell the truth! I wanna know where you've been!"

"Let you know the truth? You can't handle the truth, so don't fuck wit' it!"

"You don't know what I can handle!"

"All right, since you want the truth, let me give you the uncut version. You and I both know that it doesn't matter how many women I fuck, you ain't goin' anywhere." He pointed to her face. "I'd have to leave yo' ass for this shit to be over, and I ain't lettin' you go. We've come too damn far for you to be falling apart. Shit happens and we have to straighten the motherfucker out—"

"Straighten what out?" She tried to wiggle free from his tight embrace.

"We are a team, so if I lose, you do too!" Doing his best to calm himself, he released his grip on her throat and roughly cupped her chin. "And I need you now more than ever. We've been together too many years to let bullshit get in between what we have."

Monday stood there, tears running down her face. She knew this was about more than what he was saying; she just didn't know what. Not wanting to deal with this any longer, Monday sniffed as she pushed his hands off her and walked away from him.

His eyes trailed behind her. Even in a moment of distress Kenyatta could never deny Monday had a beautiful body. He watched her nipples protrude through her flesh-colored bra as she crawled back into bed.

"Monday, I need you."

Silence.

"You have nothing to say?"

She didn't answer and instead placed her sleep mask over her eyes and turned away from him.

As Monday settled her head into the goose-down pillow, Kenyatta went into the master bath, removed his clothes, and stepped into the shower.

As the water slid over his broad shoulders, he thought about all of the things that had happened last night.

He'd called in his cleanup guy, Tracy, an ex-cop on his personal payroll whom he'd hooked up with promotions and kickbacks, to come over to the scene and clean up everything: mop up the blood and move the body.

Perhaps whoever killed Eve really wanted him dead and she just happened to be there. Then there was the question of how they'd gotten into the apartment, when they'd gotten there, and how they even knew the apartment existed when it wasn't even leased in his name.

He knew he had enemies: the disgruntled employee, Charlie, he'd fired because Charlie didn't know how to shut the fuck up and questioned the city's deficit and budget just a little too much, the whistle-blowing cop Kenyatta had fired because he told the media how the state police in Jersey arrested Kenyatta at a Korean sex parlor and that he used the city's money to pay for the coverup.

Kenyatta swallowed and a million questions took over his mind. He let the water stream over his bald head and run down his face and body. After drowning in his thoughts a half-hour too long he turned the water off, walked out of the shower, and wrapped the bottom half of his body in a plush white towel.

Monday's back faced him when he returned to the bedroom. It was daylight, but only a small portion of the sun shone into the room and on the bed because the curtains were drawn.

She could hear him coming behind her. She shut her eyes tight because she wasn't in the mood to argue and she wasn't in the mood to think; she just wanted to be left alone.

"Monday," he whispered, his warm breath hitting the base of her neck. He ran his hands along the side of her thick hour-glass frame and began to kiss down the center of her back. Though his kisses felt good, she was determined not to let him know. Besides, these were the same lips that had probably been off last night caressing his mistress.

"Don't," Monday said, shaking her head.

"Don't fight it." He slid his wet and warm tongue down the center of her back and started pulling off her bikini panties with his teeth, his lips sliding down her butt cheeks. Her mind and her mouth were resistant, but her body was insistent and her hips lifted just enough for him to pull her underwear all the way down over her feet and toss them to the floor. He turned her over toward him and slid her bra straps off her shoulders. "Monday." He squeezed her nipples and kissed the left side of her neck. Slipping her sleep mask off, he said, "I'm your man and I need you to ride this with me."

"But I don't even know," she said as he slid his fingers into her slippery slope, "what I'm riding anymore. You don't love me."

"I love the hell outta you. Let me tell you something." He massaged her clit while looking her dead in the eyes. "You think I'm going to let something come between me and you?" He took her bra off and held her breasts together, alternating the kisses he gave her nipples. He continued to whisper, "We've been . . . together . . . for ten years," in between words he sucked her breasts, "built . . . our . . . whole life . . . together." She could feel his hardness pressed against her thigh as he untied the towel from around his waist.

She ached with desire as he cupped her breasts with his palms and slid down her belly.

Monday wanted desperately to fight against how good she felt as his tongue rocked her body, but she couldn't.

"I don't deserve you." He danced on her jumping clit with the tip of his tongue. "You've been perfect, and I haven't been all that you needed me to be." He licked.

"I owe everything to you," Kenyatta continued, his tongue feeling like sweet heat. "And if you think I'm going to let something fuck up my marriage, then you're wrong." He sucked her cream as if it were butter melting in his mouth. Never had he handled her clit as methodically as he did now. She pulled on the corner of the sheet and started to moan then scream.

"That's right, baby," he said with assurance. "Scream. I want you to scream. This is my cream." He licked inside her.

"This is all my cream." He sucked her candy until his mouth was sticky and full.

"Kenyatta," Monday moaned.

"What you want baby—tell me?"

A million thoughts of how she needed to push this mother-fucker off of her and simply bounce ran through her mind. Monday knew she didn't need to analyze, she didn't need to wonder why, how, or where all of this went wrong; she simply needed to gather what she could and leave. But she couldn't, and it was nothing she could do or knew how to do; especially with her pussy turning to orgasmic pudding in his mouth.

He blew up and down her soaking lips, taking his tongue and licking the butterscotch juice from each of them; making her thighs shake like butterflies and the muscles in her shins tighten like spasms. Monday wondered if she'd always have a Jones for him or if she'd be able to find a way to break away and detox on her own. But as he flipped her over, tossed her salad, and ran his pulsating dick over her plump ass, over her slit, and between her erotic lips she knew at this moment she would forever be addicted.

She braced the edge of the bed and winced as they eased into what had become one of their favorite positions and began fucking her with such force and speed that it was evident he was on a mission.

"This what you wanted?" He reached his hand under her belly and cupped her breasts. "Look how wet this shit is, and you tryna act like you can do without this dick."

Monday continued to fight with silence, but the screams deriving from the base of her throat were taking over. Not to mention that the slapping of his balls across her ass caused her whole body to shiver and melt into creamy pieces.

"Fuck!" Kenyatta bit his bottom lip, doing his best to change his focus from the nut rushing to his tip and instead concentrate on teaching her a lesson. He could feel Monday's pelvis begin to contract as she arched her back and threw her ass directly in the pit of his shaft.

A wicked smile ran across his face, "Oh, you want this dick now?"

Monday didn't respond, instead her body battled with her mouth's involuntary moaning and groaning.

"Tell me you want it."

The battle continued.

"Say it!"

Despite her fight, she was losing like hell, as lustful ooohes and ahhhhs forced their way through her stubborn throat.

"Say it." He stroked, pounding her in a heated succession. Nothing.

"Oh, you wanna act like you don't appreciate a mother-fucker. Ai'ight," he sniffed, "since you don't give a fuck . . ." he hit her with one last stroke and then pulled out.

"Stop playing." Monday turned over on her back, grabbed his dick, slid it back in, and gyrated her hips.

"I knew you wanted this dick. Now *tell me* you want it."

Silence.

"I swear yo' ass is stubborn. I see I'ma have to slide out again." He started to pull toward the base.

"Uhmmm . . . Kenyatta . . . don't . . . pull out . . ."

"You want this dick?"

She hesitated. "Yes."

"Say it, like you mean it!"

"I want it."

"Of course you do. Now say it again." He flipped her back around doggy style; placing his hands at the small of her back. He stroked her rapidly and just as he began to lose his breath he pulled her to the edge of the bed, forcing her head to hang off and before Monday knew it her hands were pressed on the floor and he was fucking her with her legs straight up in the air. "I'm listening," he said, holding her by the waist.

Her pussy thumped, her ass jumped, and the blood rushed to

her head. She was practically in tears, and though she hesitated, she felt dick whipped enough to say it. "I want it."

"I know you do," he said as he pulled her back on the bed and they resumed doggy style again. He bit her on the shoulders and held his hands at the base of her neck. Loving the confining position he'd put her in, his nut threatened to escape as he pushed his expanding manhood as deep as he could, filling her tight walls with every thick and uncircumcised inch of him.

His hard strokes grinded into her as her breasts flopped wildly, her hard nipples swung in the wind, and her arched back curled under his defined chest. "Listen at that shit." They became extremely silent as the noise of her pussy juices clapped against his ramming hard dick as if it were giving him a standing ovation.

"This shit wetter than a motherfucker." He spat as sweat drizzled down his chest and onto her back. "This my pussy and don't you ever forget that shit."

Monday didn't know what was better: having to submit to such pleasurable punishment or the fact that his big dick roughly hit the spot every time, causing her feelings to rewind and reconsider all the times she thought about leaving this selfish motherfucker.

Jolts of electricity forced milk to gush from between her thighs as tears slid from her eyes and her mouth hung open. All she could think was there had to be a law against a niggah like this having a dick game so intense.

As he stroked Monday, her thick cum coating his hard and luscious member, he whispered in her ear, "Tell me you love this dick."

She didn't respond.

Kenyatta stopped midstroke, "Oh, you don't love this dick?" He pounded her with all he had, his strokes intensifying as he yanked her hair back. "Answer me!" He tore into her, his strokes echoing like a whip being flicked. "Answer me! Answer . . . me!"

"Yes!" Monday screamed. She knew the bottom of her pussy had fallen out. She felt bruises form on her ass as she threw her hips onto his shaft, "I love it!"

"You better." His pace raced.

Monday didn't respond, she was too busy enjoying the whipping between her thighs. She grabbed her clit, squinted her eyes, and toyed with it.

"You ridin' for me?" Kenyatta's nut thumped at the tip of his dick like an oozing heartbeat. He did what he could to hold back his erotic explosion, but the sweetness of Monday's pussy was fucking with him and taunting him to bring it all home.

As the chilling sensation rocked Monday's body, her head started to spin. She could feel another and more powerful orgasm tumbling and wrestling in the pit of her belly, ready to bathe him with a slick coating of vanilla.

Monday began to pant and although she didn't want to, she had to call his name, because the way he was fucking her now was straight insane, "Kenyaaaaaaatttttttaaaaaa!!!" Instantly she felt her brain freeze, causing her to breathe like an asthmatic. She did what she could to get it together and collect her thoughts as she considered that maybe . . . maybe he did love her . . . and maybe . . . just maybe . . . his dick was worth all the drama he was causing . . . and maybe she needed to fall back, but whatever the maybe was, it ain't have shit on the thunderous storm of hailing cum he was now raining over her back.

Once they were done and they both lay there, Kenyatta twirled Monday's hair and said, "We're going to get through this, baby."

"Really?" she asked him, for once he sounded sincere.

"Of course. Without you, where would I be? In the streets somewhere campaigning for somebody else, not achieving my goals, steadily trying to find myself? If anything I need to say thank you. Thank you for being there, for supporting me, for encouraging me. Thank you for making me who I am today."

Monday lay on her back as he slid down her body and hooked her legs over his shoulders. She realized this was the same shit all over again. Nothing had changed, not even for a split second, and the only thing new were the scratches she'd just discovered on his back.

THREE

Collyn was caught completely off guard and slightly embarrassed as she shifted in her seat. She sat in the outdoor
café and watched her party step out of his onyx Navigator and click the remote to lock his doors. Had she known
Kenyatta's friend would be this fine, she would've rocked
her virgin-white Marilyn Monroe dress with no panties
underneath.

New York City's midmorning traffic seemed to halt as
he walked his fine ass across the street and looked directly
into her face. Though they'd only spoken on the phone,
she knew he'd recognized her as soon as he slid his avia-
tor shades off and his dimples lit up the sky.

Squeezing her inner thighs together, Collyn blew a

slow string of air out the side of her mouth as the hostess led him to their table.

He smiled at her. "Collyn?" Immediately and without hesitation, his eyes fucked every part of her curvaceous body. For a moment she wondered if that's how her name would roll off his tongue if he were stroking her.

"Bless?" She held her hand out, and he kissed it.

"Yes," he said in a smooth, deep voice. Chills shot up her spine and into her chest, causing her to arch her back, which made her breasts bounce just enough to command attention.

He was six-two and resembled the actor Idris Elba, but with a cut-up body like the rapper Fifty Cent. Just the sight of him made her already protruding nipples so hard they became sore. He was the color of pure Colombian cocoa, and his eyes were like slits of brown diamond with a natural flicker and intensity that said he was always on guard. He wore his hair in a dark faded Caesar with an abundance of spinning waves. A neatly lined boxed beard graced the flawless skin on his face.

He was dressed in an ecru Armani short-sleeve shirt, matching dress pants, and square-toe gators. His muscles tumbled down his long defined arms, and Collyn could only imagine that kissing them would flavor her lips with the essence of dark chocolate.

Collyn pushed her oval Chanel shades to the top of her head, and Bless licked his bottom lip. Just when he'd thought she couldn't get any prettier, she did. Shaped like a special-edition bottle of Coca-Cola Classic, she had the beauty of a Brazilian goddess. Her hair fell over her shoulders and to the small of her back in an abundance of sexy curls. Her skin was the color of rich mahogany, and her almond-shaped eyes spoke volumes. Her breasts were succulent, full, and perfectly round, and her killer smile was framed by kissable lips. "You're late," she said.

"And you're fine, but you don't see me complaining." He smiled, showing a perfect set of white teeth.

Collyn laughed as her eyes ran over the menu.

"What's so funny?" he asked, sitting down.

"That pathetic-ass line."

"Pathetic?" He gave her a crooked grin. "Well, would you like to suggest another one, then?"

"Not particularly." She batted her eyelashes. "But what I would like to know," she said, the tone of her voice quickly becoming serious, "is where is Kenyatta, and why would he send you alone?"

"Do you have something against being alone with me?"

"No, I have something against not knowing you, because this is not how I conduct business, and Kenyatta knows that. I would've shut this whole motherfucker down," she said, "if I knew he would be nowhere around."

"Damn, beautiful, chill. He called me right before I got here and said an emergency came up last night and he wouldn't be able to make it."

"He told you this?" she asked suspiciously.

"Yes."

"So why didn't he call me?"

"I don't know." Bless pulled out his cell phone. "Call and ask him."

Collyn stared at Bless. He was fine, but at this moment that didn't mean shit. This was not how she handled things at Red Light Special, her exclusive call-girl business, and she wasn't going to start today. She only took clients by referral and personal introductions. But not only was she feeling this niggah, she'd broken at least three of her cardinal rules when she should've dismissed his ass at hello.

She pulled out her cell phone and dialed Kenyatta's number. "Excuse me, sir," she sarcastically said to Bless as Kenyatta answered the phone. She stood up and walked away from the table. "Where are you?"

"Listen—"

"And don't lie either."

"You want me to answer the questions or not?" Kenyatta snapped.

"Hurry up."

"Bless is going to front you my half for the party, but I won't be able to make it to Sag Harbor."

"Why?"

"Everything is a mess right now."

"Like what?"

"I can't talk about it."

"You better get to fuckin' talkin' or this whole party is a wrap! Now who is this cat Bless?"

"A friend of mine. I met him a while back. He's cool. He likes hoes and shit. He wanted to give a pussy extravaganza with me and he had the money to do it, so—"

"I really have a problem with this."

"Collyn, all money is green."

"But I don't know this motherfucker."

"Look, I just told you he was straight. And I can't keep talking because some of my staff just came in."

"Kenyatta . . . Kenyatta?" When he didn't answer, Collyn realized he'd hung up on her. "Damn it!" she spat, snapping her phone shut. Still feeling uneasy, she headed back to the table.

"Done throwing a temper tantrum?" Bless asked as she sat down.

"Temper tantrum?" She cut her eyes at him. "Let me put you on notice real quick: I'm not in the mood for no bullshit.

So be clear, I don't feel like checkin' no fine-ass wanna-be-an-around-da-way niggah because he thinks he's the one.

"This is about business, and if you ain't talking about my money or trying to tell me why Kenyatta would be planning this exclusive-ass party with you and suddenly have some shit he can't discuss come up, then I don't wanna hear it! So"—she wiggled her right hand, the canary diamond she wore on her index finger sparkling in the sun—"relax that shit." She looked at the waitress, who'd just arrived at the table. "May I have a cup of coffee with a kiss of cream, please?"

"And the gentleman?" The waitress smiled.

"Just give me a minute," Bless said in a tone that let the waitress know he needed her to leave. As she walked away he cleared his throat. "Check this, beautiful." He looked at Collyn and paused. "Don't get this Armani-dress-pants outside-café shit fucked up. I'ma Brooklyn-hoodie-and-Timbs niggah all day.

"So all that rah-rah you bringin' ain't even for you. Me and ol' boy are cool, but he's not my motherfuckin' problem, so you handle that. Now, if you don't do business with people you've never met face-to-face, you should've told me that on the phone. But I'm here now and all that other shit you poppin' at the mouth is extra, so stop it. Understand?" Slipping the menu from her hands, he stroked her cheek. Running his right thumb across her MAC-covered lips, he repeated himself. "Understand?"

Collyn didn't know what turned her on the most, being put in her place or the boldness of his touch. But no matter what, she had to keep her composure. She moved his thumb and popped her lips as she spoke. "Don't touch me if I didn't give you permission to. Now . . ." She paused. "Do *you* understand?"

Before Bless could respond, Collyn's cell phone rang. She

looked at the caller ID and saw it was one of her clients in California. "Hello?" she said. "Eve didn't what? Didn't show up? . . . Yes, I will take care of this, and I will send someone else today. My apologies." She ended the call. "Look, I have to go," she said to Bless. "I have some business to take care of."

"But you're taking care of business now."

"No, I'm not. I don't know what type of games you all are playing, but I tell you what: you and Mr. Smith"—she pursed her lips—"can keep your fuckin' grip." She tucked her clutch under her arm and stood up.

"Sit yo' ass down," Bless said sternly, never raising his voice. Collyn looked at him, obviously taken aback. "I said"—he squinted as the waitress sat the coffee on the table and shot them a nervous smile—"sit down."

Reluctantly Collyn complied as the waitress walked swiftly away.

Bless leaned in toward Collyn, his lips practically touching hers. "What's really good with you, beautiful? Because this is far beyond us obviously wanting to fuck. I've got a lot of money and prestigious people tied into this who are flying in from all over, and if this doesn't go off, they're going to be pissed. Now, I don't have the time nor the patience to pacify yo' diva-ass fit. What I need is for you to keep your part of the bargain. You can get with Kenyatta later, but right now you need to deal with me."

Collyn blinked. "Bless, is it? Let me explain something to you . . . *again*," she said, looking directly into his face, her warm breath bouncing off his lips. "I'm not the one you need to play with. And ol' boy should've told you that. I'm about my business, not fucking you."

He looked at her and they locked eyes. "It's all good, beautiful. I wouldn't charge you." He seductively licked his bottom lip and slid a large envelope filled with two hundred thousand dollars across the table between them. "Now, lovely, what you gon' do?"

"About fucking you or this business arrangement?"

"Both."

Collyn sat still for a few moments. She'd been in business a long time but had never had to deal with anything like this. Although she had a good feeling about Bless, at this moment she wasn't sure if it was her aching pussy or her mind assuring her that he was straight.

Collyn's mother had passed her the torch of being an exclusive pimp handling only elite and wealthy dick—politicians, Hollywood stars, Fortune 500 CEOs, and music moguls, men with more to lose than their sorry-ass wives. And in a situation like this her mother would've told her to use her intuition and think about her reputation. To be stern, but be a lady and maintain her professionalism. And to know that if she ever canceled an event, then it better be for the right reasons. Otherwise her reputation would be at stake, and in this business reputation was everything.

Collyn leaned back in her chair and crossed her legs. "Don't let this happen again."

"Why would it?"

She didn't respond; instead she slid the envelope into her purse.

"Now," Bless said with a smile, "we can have brunch."

"Fuck brunch." She placed fifty dollars on the table to cover her coffee and tip, slid her shades back on, and flipped open her cell phone. She called her driver, and when he answered she said, "You can come around now."

Collyn stood and could feel Bless watching her ass as she strolled toward the black town car. The driver opened the rear door, and within seconds they disappeared into the city that never sleeps.

YOU HAVE MANAGED . . .

FOUR

The amber sun turned crimson as it set over the Sag Harbor estate. From what Collyn could see, the party was going to go off perfectly, from the illuminated orange paper lanterns to the tropical fish swimming in the pond to the blossoming trees swaying in the warm breeze. Directly on the shore were rows of round tables covered with white linen cloths and complemented by gold chairs. There were white-gloved butlers everywhere serving Alaskan snow crab, Maine lobster, freshly rolled sushi, filet mignon, wine, and chilled Moët. White balloons and firecrackers flew through the air, while waterfalls flowed directly into the three inground pools.

Collyn and her top girls arrived in a line of red Phantoms, and immediately all eyes were on them, which was no surprise because every actor, performer, and politician who was there knew that Collyn had the baddest chicks in the business: all brick houses, striking, voluptuous, in an array of beautiful blackness, from lusciously sweet vanilla to deep sensual chocolate.

Each stepped out of her respective Rolls and onto the thick red carpet, which was outlined by lit bamboo torches. The raging orange and blue flames created a mysterious hue that glistened off the women's statuesque bodies. Collyn's women wore only shimmering body oil and six-inch Jimmy Choos. Collyn was the exception—she wore a strapless, fitted cream silk dress that clung to her body like papier-mâché.

Collyn looked over her girls as French horns sounded and exotic male escorts took them by the arm and led them to their assigned venues for the night.

Once all the girls had dispersed Collyn strolled the grounds. Though she never participated in any of the sex, it was her job to ensure that everyone here had their fantasies fulfilled. And nothing was off-limits. By the time the guests left here all of their fantasies would be reality.

Each enclosed white tent had been assigned a different theme: girl on girl, swinging, voyeurism, threesomes, foursomes, and anything else one could imagine.

"Champagne?" the butler asked her, as she exited the S&M tent.

"Thank you." She lifted a glass of Moët from the gold tray.

"Collyn."

She turned around and noticed one of her regular and politically affiliated clients calling her name.

"Peterson, hello." They kissed each other on each cheek.

"How've you been?" he pointed to Bless, who was standing next to him. "Are you familiar with Blessing Shields?"

She nodded her head, "Pleasure."

He smiled, looking her over, "I'm sure."

Immediately Collyn's clit jumped. "So how have things been, Peterson?" Collyn said as she tapped the ball of her stiletto, hoping that no one could feel the force of her involuntary pussy pumps. She was half heartedly listening to Peterson as her eyes drifted toward staring at Bless. Never had she seen a man so beautiful: the butterfly muscles that protruded from his collarbones and ran into his defined arms were like exquisite works of African art.

He wore a tight wife-beater that complimented his washboard abs and large pecs. His beige linen pants hung off his waist, hinting at the defined ass within—one that she could imagine grabbing while they made love.

Collyn traced the rim of the glass with the tip of her index finger as she wondered how salty his skin would taste.

Damn, Collyn thought, *this shit is crazy. I know better than this.* "Well, Peterson, Blessing. It's been very nice chatting with you, but if you'll excuse me." She turned around, "And Peterson," she threw over her shoulder, "I just spotted your favorite girl, going into your favorite fetish tent."

"Excuse me, Bless." Peterson said as Collyn made her way back around the grounds. She was pissed that whatever attraction she had for Bless, she couldn't seem to shake. Yeah she loved men and treasured dick, but no matter how rich he appeared to be, he was a trick, and the number one rule that her mother raised her with was tricks were off-limits.

Making her way through the half-naked crowd, Collyn sat down at the makeshift bar under the tent where there was live dance hall music. Although this was a high-class orgy, with people having their fetishes fulfilled all around them, the crowd in here was clothed. This was the one place the guests could go if they were taking an intermission from fucking and wanted to get their swerve on.

"You drinkin' or thinkin'?" the bartender asked her.

She smiled, "Both."

"Well," he said, "I can listen to one and go get the other."

"Well, thank you." Collyn laughed. "But I'll just have another glass of Moët." She slid back on the stool and enjoyed the music.

The music reminded her of Kingston, Jamaica, her mother's hometown. She closed her eyes and envisioned herself walking through the Caribbean sand. As she heard the bartender pouring her drink, "Thinking about me?" poured over her shoulder. She knew it was Bless.

"Not quite," she snapped.

"You're too pretty to lie."

Collyn laughed. She hated that he was so persistent, because it made it that much harder to resist him.

"So, do I get this dance?" he asked.

"I don't mix business and pleasure."

"Ai'ight, then place me on the side of pleasure."

"I can't do that."

"Why not?"

"Because I'm the only one here who's not for sale."

"Give it to me for free."

Collyn crossed her legs, her erotic pearl pounding like a drumbeat. "And suppose I have a man?"

He spun her around toward him. "Fuck your man."

Dead silence. There was nothing much to say after that. At least nothing Collyn could think of right away. She looked in his face and could see he was undressing every part of her body . . . *again.*

To him she was stunning, and every luscious curve of her exceeded perfection. Bless could only imagine that holding her in his arms would be the epitome of giving him something he could feel. Unable to resist, he slid his index finger down her full cleavage.

"Didn't I tell you about touching me?" Collyn warned.

"You want me to stop?"

After a moment of dead silence Collyn said, "Look, there's a lot of pussy out there and you paid a lot of money to have it here, so why don't you go and enjoy?"

"Do you really want me to go out there and fuck one of them?" He gazed into her eyes and stroked her cheek.

Although Collyn found herself envisioning Bless's smooth lips wrapping around her thick nipples, she didn't respond to his question. There was no way he realized what he was asking her to compromise. Acting on his gesture and giving into the electricity of his warm touch heated her body with would've gone against every principle she ran her business with. But perhaps this wasn't about business.

Collyn grabbed his hand and led him to the dance floor. Though she had on four-inch stilettos, he was still significantly taller than her.

Lady Saw's "Chat to Mi Back" was playing and the dance floor was packed.

The tent was air-conditioned, yet the beat of the music and the dance movements made the cool air nonexistent. Collyn placed her arms around Bless's neck and he rested his hands on her waist.

"You like to run, huh?" he asked her.

"What are you talking about?" Her dance moves proved that she was every bit West Indian as her hips whined with ease.

"You feeling the hell outta me and you runnin' like crazy."

She didn't respond. Instead she turned around and whined onto his shaft. His hard dick was a perfect fit down the middle of her slit. As her hands practically touched the ground Bless couldn't help but feel her luscious behind, and that's when he discovered she didn't have any panties on. He placed his hands beneath her dress and his middle finger slipped through her wetness. "Shit," he said as his finger became slick.

Collyn stood up straight, turned around, sucked the candy off his fingertip, and resumed dancing. "I will let you know when it's time to put your fingers there," she said seductively.

"I wanna put more than my finger there." Bless pulled her to him and her hips moved as if they were remote controlled by his large hands, which glided up and down the sides of her thighs. He buried his nose in the side of her neck, lightly kissing her collarbones, sucking her chin, moving on to her lips. Surprisingly, she didn't stop him. Nor did she want to stop him, the magnetism of his touch seduced her into letting him finish.

As the music continued to play, Collyn found herself exhaling as Bless's tongue traveled deeply into her mouth. Never had she been kissed like this. A kiss like this is what caused the fear of falling in love to either subside or come alive. Bless backed Collyn into a secluded corner of the tent and pulled her dress up. "Stop," she said, while continuing to kiss him. "I'm not doing this." She broke their lip-lock, her stiff nipples pressed against his chest.

"Ai'ight." He forced himself to stop, his hard dick ready to bust. He took a few moments to calm down before he said anything. "So when I'ma see you again?"

"I think it's best"—she straightened her dress—"if we don't."

"Why not?"

"Because . . ." She paused. "You're . . . a client and that's what's best. We've already gone too far—"

"Really?"

"Yes. Really and—"

"Collyn—"

"—and I just think—"

"Beautiful," he said with ease, "all that shit you sayin', you don't even believe it." Bless reached in his side pocket, pulled out a Cuban cigar, lit it, and blew smoke from the side of his mouth.

"We can be friends, Bless," she said.

"Friends?" He arched his eyebrows. "So we niggahs now?"

"I guess."

"You guess? I was two seconds from fucking the shit outta you and you lookin' at me and sayin' we niggahs? That you my dude?"

"Exactly," she said confidently. "I mean, if you can't handle it, then that's not my problem."

"If you good, ma, then I'm good."

"Ai'ight . . . so, straight."

"Fa' sho," he said, ending the conversation, "but let me show you what I do with my boys."

"What?"

He gave her a pound. "I'm out." And he left her standing there.

FIVE

The red numbers from the clock radio flashed 8:00 A.M. like breaking news across the middle of the bedroom's three floor-to-ceiling windows as Kenyatta's heavy eyes begged him to close them. For the last month, he'd been fighting to stay awake, doing his all to keep Eve's dead body out of his dreams. If he slept, that image caused him to wake up every morning in a cold sweat, screaming.

He looked toward Monday, who was sound asleep, then eased out of the bed, grabbed his cell phone, and headed into the bathroom, where he called Tracy. "Tracy," he whispered, peeking back at Monday before walking over to the bathroom window and looking out at the grounds, "did you find out anything?"

"Nothing," Tracy said.

"Fuck!" Kenyatta snapped. "I need this shit taken care of. Every day I'm paranoid as hell."

"We should have something soon. And I'll call you when we do."

"Please." Kenyatta hung up, and when he turned around Monday was standing there. He jumped and dropped his phone on the floor. "What the fuck you sneaking up on me for?"

"Sneaking up on you?" Monday said, taken aback. "You're the one walking around here all nervous and shit."

"I don't have anything to be nervous about."

"I can't tell. Kenyatta, why don't you just tell me what's going on with you? I promise I will understand. I will. Let's just talk about this."

Kenyatta stared at Monday. He thought about how he'd cheated on her a thousand times, had sideline babies, lied, borrowed the "I love you" line that he'd promised was only for her and spat it at bitches who didn't mean shit. He knew this level of cheating had to be a disorder, perhaps something he'd been born with.

He'd always loved sex and would try mostly anything, which is why he embarked on the venture of paying for pussy, because he wanted to see if the ill na na was sweeter when it had a price than when it was free.

Kenyatta knew by the hurt lining Monday's eyes that no matter how much of a lover, homie, and friend she wanted to be, she couldn't handle the realness of it. "Monday, I'm not in the mood to be questioned."

Monday sucked her teeth and stormed away.

• • •

Two hours later, after their morning showers, they were both dressed and back to their daily routine.

"What do you mean City Council vetoed my bill?" Kenyatta

paced the floor and spat into the phone as Monday walked into his home office and stood in the doorway stunned. Her stomach tightened and she saw everything they'd worked for flash before her eyes. Kenyatta was on the phone, squinting his lips tight and taking steady pulls of weed while he discussed city business with his financial secretary.

"And what are you doing?" Monday plopped his leather briefcase on his desk. "Is there a secret desire to be Marion Barry?"

"Crack is whack," he placed his hand over the receiver, "this is weed." He took a pull and blew the smoke toward her face.

"You look ridiculous." She peered at him, "You have to prepare for a meeting with City Council this morning and all you can think to do is get high? Am I even seeing this?" she raised her hands above her eyes like a sun visor, "Is this even for real?"

Kenyatta looked at the burning tip of weed and then stuck the opposite end back into his mouth. "Look I'm going through something right now." He resumed his telephone conversation. "I understand what you're saying Elijah, but I need that bill rewritten because this budget has to be passed. We told the superintendent that we would raise the budget for the existing schools and look into building new ones. This has to be passed." He paused, took another pull, and said, "They don't need to worry," he blew smoke from the corner of his lips, "about the city's budget. Look, just have the minutes from the meeting typed up and ready for me when I reach City Hall this morning."

And as he hung up Monday said, "I just hope whatever bitch that has you losing it isn't pregnant." She picked up the Febreze and sprayed. "Put that away." She fanned her hand.

"Excuse me," the maid said as she stepped into his office.

She noticed Kenyatta smoking weed and immediately stepped back out and knocked on the door frame, "May I . . . uhhh . . . come in?"

"Damn Mary." Kenyatta said as if he'd just remembered she'd worked here. He hurriedly mashed the joint in the ashtray and sprayed Febreze all over himself and into the air. "Yeah, Mary," he arched his back and popped a peppermint in his mouth. "Good morning. How are you?"

"Fine, sir, and yourself?"

"Couldn't be better."

"Well, Ms. Hudson James is here."

"Let her know that I'll be out in a moment."

"She says she needs to see you now, sir."

"Tell her I said—"

"Thank you, Mary," Hudson said as she walked into his office. She stood still and sniffed. The longer side of her mid-length bob swayed as she moved her neck from side to side. The corners of her mouth curled in disgust, causing her smooth coffee-colored skin to wrinkle. She looked at Monday and then to Kenyatta.

"Know what?" she said, closing the office door. "We have more important things to deal with." Hudson slammed down two newspapers. She pointed to one of the headlines and began to read: " 'Missing Woman Had an Affair with Mayor Kenyatta Smith.' "

Monday felt woozy, while Kenyatta blinked. "What the hell is this?" he questioned in disbelief.

"It's exactly what it looks like." Hudson picked up the next newspaper. "The missing woman, Eve Johnson, was Senator Edward Reign's sister-in-law. His wife is distraught and claims her sister called her daily and told her about an affair with the mayor."

"I knew it was some bullshit," Monday said, dazed.

Kenyatta stared off into space and then turned back to Hudson. "Release a written statement saying it isn't true."

"Not good enough. You need more than a written statement."

"Who the fuck is Eve Johnson?" Monday screamed.

"It's a long story."

"Make it short."

"It was nothing. The paper's lying." He looked her in the eyes.

Monday glanced at his twitching jaw. "You're lying."

"Not now, Monday."

"Then when?"

"Hudson," Kenyatta said, ignoring Monday, "why isn't a written statement good enough?"

"Because, Mayor, you are dealing with a very well-respected senator who's already not a fan of your politics. And now his wife's favorite sister is not only missing in your city but also is reported to have raved about an affair with you. A written statement isn't good enough; you have to hold a press conference."

Kenyatta glared. "Hell no! We weren't lovers."

Monday stared Kenyatta directly in the face and hated that she knew when he was lying. She hated it because underneath all of the superficial bullshit that stopped her from letting go, she needed another reason besides a possessed penis to stay.

Hudson looked at her watch. "I'll schedule the press conference for an hour from now. And Monday"—Hudson looked at her—"would you like me to go upstairs with you so you can change? Preferably into a gray or navy blue two-piece modest suit and pearls. We can also rehearse what you need to do and how wide you need to smile while you're standing at his side on TV."

"TV?" Monday was in disbelief at the thought of being one of those political wives standing by their man while he was sinking in quicksand.

"Yes, TV. It's important that you're there. It gives more credence to the mayor's commitment to finding Eve."

Coming out of disbelief and no longer speechless, Monday spat, "Do you hear what you're asking me to do? TV? After what I just found out? Are you serious? I don't give a fuck if they never find the bitch." She pointed to the paper.

Hudson looked at Monday, taken aback. "Please don't say that again. Let's save the 'mad black woman' fits for after the cameras have been packed up, as going off on TV is not an option. You have to do it. Oh—and I just thought of this—while you're on the air, I want you to make a statement to the family."

"What?"

"Yes, tell the family that as a wife and member of this community, you are sorry for their misfortune and their time of turmoil. It would seem more sincere coming from a woman than a man. And make your voice tremble a bit, so that the viewers can sense your compassion."

"Wonderful idea." Monday batted her eyelashes. "And maybe I should say," she went on, enunciating every word, "that I sincerely hope your dearly beloved, home-wrecking, two-timing ho-ass bitch of a loved one is dead when she's found."

Kenyatta stood stunned for a moment and his knees buckled. "Excuse us." Kenyatta turned to Hudson.

"What?" Hudson asked. "We need to deal with this."

"I said excuse us. As a matter of fact, I'll meet you at City Hall."

Grudgingly Hudson walked out the door. Once she was gone, Kenyatta turned back to Monday, who spat at him. "Were you fuckin' that missing-ass bitch?"

Kenyatta sighed. "Monday," he said softly, holding her hands between his, "listen, baby. I know you're upset and hurt—"

"Oh, you know this? So tell me, were you fucking her?"

"No."

She looked at his jaw to see if it would twitch, and when it didn't, she asked, "Did you know her?"

Kenyatta paused. "I met her once. That's it, but it was nothing. I don't even remember what she looks like."

"So the paper is just making shit up. Out of all the mayors in New York state, this bitch nails Kenyatta Smith as her man."

"Look, I know it sounds bad, which is why I'm going to do this press conference. I promise that after the conference we can talk about this as much as you want. But right now I need you at my side, for your support as well as our political image."

"Political image? That's what this is about?"

"Monday—"

"Fuck your political image!"

"What?" He took a step back. "We have to do this for the public." It was evident that staying calm was trying. "Image is everything in politics, and you know it."

"How about this? I will not be going on TV! Not Monday. Not this motherfuckin' Monday anyway. So you, the public, and that missing bitch can kiss my extra-wide black ass." Monday slapped herself on her left butt cheek for emphasis.

Kenyatta snatched Monday by the arm. "Understand this: you will do it." His hot breath ran along the side of her neck. "And you will do it because you don't have a choice. All of that singsong shit is a front you puttin' on for your damn self. Now, I understand that you're hurt, and like I said, we will deal with that later. But right now you will be about your business. I don't want to hear any more complaining about what you are and are not going to do, because right now that's not an option. Do you understand me?"

Silence.

"I said, do you understand me?"

Monday snatched her arm away. "Fuck you!"

• • •

Flashing lights from the sea of cameras danced in Monday's eyes as she wondered what everyone present thought of her. She didn't quite know what to make of herself as she stood side by side with Kenyatta, looking somberly at a man she so desperately wanted to spit on. She gave a half smile and nodded as one of the journalists called her name and snapped her picture when she turned around.

Kenyatta cleared his throat and the crowd of media started to quiet down. He stood behind the podium with his back straight, looking cool and confident. His round gold-framed glasses rested on the bridge of his nose, and his gray double-breasted suit was pressed to perfection. He looked directly into the camera and began to speak. "I come humbly before you not only as the mayor of our great city but also as a man who is very hurt by the allegations that I was having an affair with Eve Johnson."

As if on cue, Monday grabbed his hand and he squeezed hers. "There have been a series of articles in which I'm being accused of knowing this poor woman. Her being missing is an unfortunate situation, but I do not know this woman. And I sincerely hope this is not a political ploy by Senator Reigns and his party." Monday blinked, and she could see Hudson and the speechwriter glaring at him. It was obvious that line hadn't been scripted. "Because if so, that is even more unfortunate, as we all know that this is not about political disagreements—this is about human life."

Kenyatta turned to Monday, who gave him a reassuring nod and a small smile. Monday swallowed, then spoke into the microphone on the podium. She could feel him rubbing her back. "I ask you to please remain as dedicated to my husband as I am." The words felt like nails leaving her mouth. He squeezed her hand, both of them knowing that that wasn't remotely close to what she was supposed to say. After an awkward moment of silence during which Kenyatta realized that Monday wasn't going to say anything more, he ended his statement by saying, "Thank you and I bid you farewell."

Monday stepped away from the podium, her eyes filled with tears. She looked behind her. Kenyatta was talking with Hudson, never once looking her way.

She continued down the hall and felt as though everyone she saw was laughing at her. That they felt about her the same way she did about herself. She wondered how many people watched her on television and said to themselves, "That's one stupid bitch." Tears clouded her eyes and her heels clicked against the waxed floors of City Hall.

Suddenly she felt as if she'd hit a brick wall, and "Slow down" floated into her face as she felt someone catch her by the arm.

"I'm sorry, I didn't see you." Monday looked up and stumbled just a bit. Not enough to fall, but enough to reveal that she was caught off-guard, "Mehki . . ."

"Are you okay?"

"Uh, yes," she said, backing out of his embrace. Monday wasn't sure what made her more uncomfortable, his prolonged embrace or her inability to stop admiring his beauty. He was that blacker-the-berry-sweeter-the-juice type beauty. The color of freshly brewed tea with eyes of a Senegalese king. He stood six-four, with the athletic build of a heavyweight champion topped off with a Denzel swagger: confident, strong, and impressive to everyone who met him, which is why Monday never truly got over him.

Once upon a time, she'd loved Mehki because her heart gave her no choice. He knew her struggles, he knew what it was to blossom from nothing, he knew what it was to dream, and to have a desire to touch the untouchable. He understood her silence, he could decipher her cries, he knew her favorite color, her favorite food, and her favorite things to do. He knew her inside and out, which is why she couldn't marry him. At the time, she needed to run away from herself and there was no way she could bring him along.

They were in their last year of undergrad and a few months from their wedding date when she'd made love to him one night and he awoke the next morning to find her engagement ring on the tip of his pinky finger and a Dear John letter on the empty side of the bed. Needless to say she never expected to see him again, let alone see him today. "What are you doing here?"

"I have a firm here . . . well, in Harlem."

"But what are you doing *here*?"

"The mayor hired me as his personal attorney."

Monday blinked. "He did what? Did you . . . know that he's my husband?"

"I do now."

"I ah, need to go."

Mehki pushed the hair on her shoulders and cupped it behind her ears. "At least this time you're letting me know up front."

Instead of responding, Monday turned on her heels and left him standing there.

SIX

Monday sipped her third glass of white wine as she stood shifting from one four-inch, strappy Yves Saint Laurent pencil heel to the other, her silver midthigh flapper dress making love to every one of her voluptuous curves.

She smiled mostly with the corners of her lips as a group of political wives discussed how much money they'd contributed to the annual pink-ribbon cancer research gala they were attending.

Though Monday acted as if she were interested in their conversation, she was really watching Kenyatta work the room with his boyish charm. She couldn't believe that no one seemed to see through his bullshit.

For a moment Monday wondered if she was the one who was insane. Hell, maybe she was Lauryn Hill and this was a sanity convention—which would explain why everyone else here was at ease. Or perhaps this was simply the epitome of democracy.

"Excuse me, Mrs. Smith," Jocelyn, the wife of the head of transportation, said to Monday. "I just want you to know that I admired the way you stood by your husband at the press conference."

Monday almost spat her drink out. She started coughing and Jocelyn handed her a tissue. "Thank you," she said with a scratchy throat.

"It was just so touching," Harriet, the chief circuit judge's wife, added her two cents.

"But of course," Jocelyn remarked, "we certainly don't believe any of those rumors."

Monday didn't have a chance to respond, as just then Hudson walked over. She smiled at the other women before pulling Monday to the side. "Kenyatta will be making a speech momentarily, so he'll need you soon."

"What the hell does he need me for?" Monday's words slurred just a little. "Shit, he's married to his dick."

Instantly the circle of women behind them gasped and erupted in snickers.

"Monday," Kenyatta, who Monday hadn't known was behind them, said, sounding surprised. He politely took the drink from her hand.

"What?" Monday snatched it back, causing the wine to stir and splash against the sides of the glass.

"Stop it," Kenyatta said tight lipped.

"Spare me."

Kenyatta cleared his throat, noticing Bless coming their way.

"Kenyatta." Bless held his hand out. "Monday, how's everything?"

"Everything is fine," Kenyatta said, shaking Bless' hand and smiling. "But Monday isn't feeling too well; she may be getting ready to leave."

"Puh-leeze, I've been thrown out of better places by worse people."

"Listen," Bless said, obviously uncomfortable, "if you have a moment, I would like to discuss the details of this new contract."

"Let's," Kenyatta said to Bless as he shot Hudson a look that told her to keep an eye on Monday.

Once they were out of earshot, Hudson turned to Monday and curled her upper lip. "I would suggest you rethink the attitude you've been displaying."

Monday continued to sip her drink.

"Monday, do you hear me?"

"Oh, I hear you, but you damn sure aren't talking to me. I might be a little tipsy, but this is not your auntie's barbecue, so watch your fuckin' mouth."

Not wanting to make a scene, Hudson put her hips in motion and walked toward Kenyatta, who was still speaking with Bless. Once Hudson was standing next to Kenyatta, Monday noticed how he softly ran his thumb across Hudson's chin. It was a small and subtle gesture that spoke volumes. Suddenly Monday sobered up. She hoped that what her mind, her eyes, and her third chakra, the one in the pit of her stomach, were telling her was mistaken. Perhaps Kenyatta's fingers running across Hudson's chin was nothing.

Monday grabbed another glass of wine from a passing tray and chugged it down in one shot. As she reached for another, Kenyatta discreetly took her by the elbow.

"Looks like somebody else'll be missing tomorrow." Jocelyn's voice drifted toward Monday as Kenyatta escorted her toward the ladies' room.

"Sir, sir," the valet stuttered, "this—this is the ladies' room."

Kenyatta slid a crisp one-hundred-dollar bill into her hand. "Excuse us, please."

The valet happily obliged, and once she left, Kenyatta locked the door behind her. "What the fuck is wrong with you?" he screamed at Monday.

"You and yo' cheatin' ass! Got bitches out there laughing at me and shit. 'Way to go,' " she said mockingly. " 'Stand by your man!' " She wiggled her neck. "No, what I should do is leave your fuckin' ass."

"Monday, please. What you need to do is sober the fuck up!"

"And you need to keep your dick in your pants! 'Cause I know you were fuckin' that Eve bitch!"

Kenyatta frowned. He'd come to hate the sound of Eve's name. "Monday, this is not the time nor the place for this shit."

"You know what? You're right. That's why I'm taking my ass home."

Kenyatta pulled Monday back to him just as a knock sounded on the door. "Excuse me. Is anyone breathing in there?" Jocelyn asked.

"We'll be out in a minute," Kenyatta called.

He held Monday to his chest. "Why are you doing this?" he said calmly, knowing that the only way to control her was to act concerned and sound sincere.

"Kenyatta, just go ahead." Monday pushed against his chest.

He grabbed her hand and held it, pressing his forehead against hers. "Baby," he said, kissing her, "calm down. Fuck them gossiping-ass bitches. They don't know what goes on in our house. They don't know how much I love you." Kenyatta kissed her as she attempted to push away.

"Kenyatta," Monday weakly protested, "let me go." He kissed her along the sides of her neck. "Let me go," she repeated.

"You really want me to let you go?" He eased his hands up her dress and rubbed between her thighs. "You're not my baby anymore?"

"Would you stop!"

"Oh what, I can't get any more of that?" He pulled her panties to the side and worked his fingers into her wetness. "I thought you said this shit would always be mine. Ain't this my pussy?" He rubbed the tip of his thumb against her clit.

"Kenyatta." She felt herself getting weak.

"Answer me." He continued to play. "Look at me and tell me it ain't mine."

"Kenyatta," she sighed, hating that this was always the moment he got exactly what he wanted. She was as addicted to giving it to him as he was to taking it. "I'm just tired of this."

"What I just tell you?" Kenyatta lifted Monday onto the black marble countertop, the length (or lack thereof) of her dress giving him full access to exactly what he wanted.

"This my pussy?" Kenyatta unzipped his pants and pulled his dick through the slit. Monday stared at Kenyatta's hardness as he slid the head slowly into her wetness, poking it against her clit and sliding it between her soft walls.

Monday gasped as he pressed her back against the mirror. Just as she started to throw a hard hip back at him, he slid his wet dick out and said, "Look at how I got you wide open." She looked at his glazed chocolate dick. Her mouth watered and she bit the inside of her cheek.

"Excuse me." There was another knock on the door, but they ignored it.

Kenyatta looked toward the door and back at Monday. He quickly slid his dick in and back out again. "Maybe I'll give this good dick to your friend out there, since you don't appreciate a niggah."

"No." Monday swallowed as jealousy pricked her pride and she tightened the grip on his waist.

"What?" He teased her with the expanding head. "I know you don't want no dick 'cause you haven't even told me this was my pussy yet."

"It's yours," she said as her legs shook. "It's yours." Monday rotated her hips, giving him full access to her sweet pinkness.

"You gon' do this shit again? Acting all crazy?"

"N-n-noooo . . . ," she stammered.

"You gon' act right?"

"Yes . . ."

"Always stressin' a niggah and shit. Told you I love you and to stop worrying about these bitches out there."

Monday's breathing sounded as if she'd run a marathon as his hard dick thrust against the back wall of her pussy, pushing it back farther and farther until she could feel it start to collapse. Her orgasm was building in her stomach as she started to pant. "I'm—I'm sorry, baby."

Kenyatta locked gazes with Monday. "I know you ain't cummin'." Kenyatta bounced her up and down on his dick. "Don't cum until I tell you to!"

Monday did her all to hold out, but she could feel the butterflies in her stomach preparing to take flight. "Baby . . ."

"What?"

"I'm—I'm cummin', I can't help it."

"You cummin', baby?" Kenyatta quickened his pace, and just as if it were fate, they both came, holding on to dear life and even tighter to each other.

Once they were done Kenyatta backed away and began fixing his clothes. Monday continued to sit on the vanity, feeling the high from having twirled her hips, clapped her pussy across his dick, and screamed his name floating away.

She knew it was only a moment before the essence of feeling fucked-up presented itself again. She was slowly withering into being insane. Especially since all of her intelligence was abandoned when it came to this irrational and unstable motherfucker.

Monday was tired. Tired of being the wife but treated like a nagging-ass mistress. Tired of being dismissed, and when she reminded him of who she was by cussin' his ass out and threatening to leave, instead of doing better he fucked her into forgetfulness.

Monday looked around the bathroom and realized Kenyatta was completely dressed and ready to go while she sat there in disheveled clothes.

"What are you waiting on?" he asked her.

"Nothing." Monday eased off the vanity, fixed her dress, and then looked in the mirror and patted the stray and loose strands of hair back in place.

"Ready?" Kenyatta asked her as he approached the door.

"Yeah." She said, stepping out of the bathroom, and as Kenyatta headed in the direction of the gala to give his speech, Monday walked toward the lobby and out the door.

SEVEN

The hot asphalt crackled beneath Collyn's tires and the summer breeze flew behind her as she whipped her candy-apple-red BMW Z3 roadster into her personal parking space at her Upper West Side art gallery. Although she was a purveyor of pussy, she was also a connoisseur of fine art: paintings, hand-carved statues, and one-of-a-kind furnishings from all over the world. The clients who bought her art pieces were just as elite as those who were serviced at her underground business.

As she pushed open the glass door, the jazz sound track playing inside provided a soothing welcome into the gallery, given all that she had on her mind. Along with being uneasy about Kenyatta and his scheming, she'd been unable to shake thoughts of Bless. Just the thought of him caused her nipples to protrude through her sky-blue sleeveless rayon blouse. The hem of her matching wide-leg pants swayed over her three-inch ocean-blue Manolos as she walked over to Taryn, her assistant and cousin, who handed her a stack of mail and said, "The mayor is in the back to see you. I had him sit in the private lounge until you came."

"Thank you, Taryn." Collyn smiled. Her heels clicked across the Italian tile floor as she walked to the back of the gallery, where her office and private lounge were located. This was where she usually met with her top Red Light Special clients.

Collyn nodded at Kenyatta as she opened the lounge's door and then led him to her office. As she closed the door behind them, Kenyatta grabbed the remote to the electric miniblinds and closed them.

"Ms. Bazemore." Kenyatta slyly looked her over.

Collyn arched her eyebrows. "Where have you been? I've been calling you for weeks!"

"Excuse me, do you think I run the city by appointment? I have a twenty-four-hour position."

"Spare me, please. All I wanna know is what the hell is going on, and what is this shit with Eve missing?"

"I was going to ask you the same thing. When's the last time you saw her?"

"The night before I paid for her plane ticket to California."

"And when was that?"

"The night before Sag Harbor."

"And what happened that night?" Kenyatta pressed. "Did you argue or something?"

Collyn frowned. "And who the fuck are you, 007? The question is when's the last time you saw her?"

Kenyatta paused as he walked around Collyn's office. "I haven't seen the bitch . . . in months."

"What?" Collyn looked at him strangely, then grabbed her BlackBerry. "Eve had an appointment with you a few weeks ago. As a matter of fact . . ." her voice trailed off as she scrolled her electronic calendar, "she had an appointment with you since July Fourth weekend."

"So what are you implying, Collyn?" he spat defensively.

"I'm not implying anything."

"Then what do you call it? Besides," he smirked, "if you saw her the night before Sag Harbor, then it seems to me you were the last person to be with her, so where is she?"

"Good question. You tell me. Because she was supposed to have been in California finishing up some of her last parties with my company and she never made it."

"Look, I don't know anything about California or anything else. All I know is that the last time we were together was months ago."

"Where'd you meet?"

"Ah . . . the Wyndham."

"I usually schedule you at the Hilton."

"No, you didn't!"

"What are you talking about? You know I did!" Collyn paused. She watched the side of his jaw twitch. "You think I'm stupid? Do I look like a fool to you?"

Kenyatta stared at Collyn. He thought about telling her the truth, but then he quickly changed his mind for all he knew Collyn could have killed Eve or had her killed. "All I know is that we had an appointment and that was it."

"And all I know is that yo' ass is lying. Which leads me to this, did you do something to her?"

"Hell, did you?!" Kenyatta spat. "Especially since everyone knew she wanted to start her own business and you were upset about her leaving."

"Do you really think I cared? As far as I'm concerned all is fair in cash and dick. I was helping her to set up her own business in California. I didn't give a damn."

"Yeah, right. And who do you think would believe you'd be so willing to have your top girl start her own business? Everyone would see right through that lie."

"And why would I have to lie to you Mayor Smith?"

"You tell me." He shrugged. "I mean really, who do you think would buy it? Everyone would know you're lying. Come on . . . what do you think the police will say about you? You ever think of how you will look in orange once they see that this art gallery is a front for the state's largest prostitution ring?"

"Interesting." Collyn smirked.

"Hey." He lifted his hands. "I'm just telling you what I think."

Collyn laughed. "Let me tell you what *I* think. I think Eve is more easily tied to you than to me. Also, I think that you are a fuckin' sex addict, a weirdo who can't control his desire for prostitutes. You're worse than a crack fiend 'cause there's no rehab for you. What happened, Kenyatta? Did your uncle, your cousin, your mother's boyfriend play with your prick and make you feel inadequate, so now you think paying for pussy gives you control? Aw, poor thing. You're still not controlling anything. Not even your own part of the government, because as quiet as it's kept, the City Council does that. So what do you control? Pussy? The hoes? When they cum? Well, let me tell you a little secret." She leaned in close to his left ear and whispered, "You don't even control that. It's the money that does. They get paid to cum—"

"Bitch, I'll—" Kenyatta raised his hand in the air.

"Do it." Collyn sat on the edge of her desk and crossed her legs. "Please." She slammed her purse on the table, and the bottom hit with a solid thud. Kenyatta knew that Collyn was never without her piece. " 'Cause that will be just the excuse I need to lay out a niggah. Now, I get it that you all paranoid and shit about where the hell this chick is, but don't try and pin no shit on me. I'm done with your ass. If you want a ho, you better skip down to Hunt's Point with the rest of the perverts."

Kenyatta leaned against the desk, "You think you're the only pussy service in town?" He gave her half a smile. "You really think I'ma go without because of you?" He laughed. "I don't think so. So I tell you what—if you fuck with me, we'll just see how long it'll be before you're on the run."

"My dear, I ain't never run from a damn thing, and I damn sure ain't going to pick today to start running. So do what you need to, because trust and believe, I am not the bitch you wanna get in the mud with!"

"So I guess we're done." He straightened his collar.

"Pretty much."

Collyn opened her office door and Kenyatta walked out.

Although she did her best to play it off, she knew that the mayor had the ability to convince the police of a lot of things, and she prayed that foul play concerning Eve's disappearance wasn't one of them.

EIGHT

Collyn closed her gallery for the evening and on the way home bought bottles of Patrón and Coke in hopes of clearing her mind of Kenyatta's antics and her growing desire for Bless.

After pulling her car in front of the building for valet parking, she waved to the doorman. "Ms. Bazemore," he said, "would you like me to carry your bag?"

"No, thank you, Bradford." She smiled as she sauntered into the glass elevator, swiped her electronic key, and headed up to her penthouse suite.

Collyn's penthouse was exquisite: her living room had twenty-foot-high cathedral ceilings, one-of-a-kind works of art hanging on crisp white walls, and a specially designed white calf-suede sectional with two hand-carved South African square tables that sat on a handwoven Persian rug. On the opposite side of the living room was a West African onyx and wood dining set that led to the wide-open and sleekly designed kitchen. Each room had panoramic views of the New York City skyline, including the master bath, which had a glass ceiling and a two-person soaking tub that sat in the middle of the heated soapstone floor.

Collyn slipped her stilettos off at the door, tossed her bag on the sectional, and mixed herself a drink. She carried her glass into her bedroom, where she turned on her CD player, removed her clothing, and slipped into a black spaghetti-strap nightie. She sat in the middle of her bed and lay back against her cashmere pillows as the sounds of Najee filled the room. For the first time since she met Bless, she wondered if she needed to stop fighting how she felt.

Not only was her attraction to him undeniable, but for the past month it had been unshakable.

Though over the years she had had men here and there, there were very few who made it to her bed, and even fewer who made it to her heart.

But then again, her mind told her, she'd been alone for so long, and she was too independent, too strong, and too selfish to give someone the time of day.

She placed her drink on the nightstand and turned over to sleep, yet as she closed her eyes, her mind lost control and her body took over. Her breasts longed to be handled by Bless—kissed, sucked, and played with. Her navel desired to have his wet, luscious tongue slide inside it and then move on to sucking up her melting sugar in intervals of sloppy kisses. She needed his stiff dick to get her grind on and knock the bottom of her pussy into oblivion. She wanted him to pull her hair, kiss her shoulders with playful bites. She wanted to wrap her hands around his thick, masculine neck and demand that he fuck the hell out of her.

Collyn slid the tickling corner of the pillow between her tingling thighs. She opened her eyes and looked at the time: eleven thirty. She couldn't fight it any longer. She knew she was taking a chance by calling, considering the way they'd left things, but she figured if he didn't answer or he didn't seem pleased to hear from her, then fuck it.

She dialed his number and the phone rang three times before he answered. "Yo," he said groggily.

"You're asleep?" Suddenly she was nervous. "I'll call you another time."

"There you go runnin' again. It's cool. I'm not asleep. Wassup?"

She smiled. She was happy he knew her voice. "It's been a while. I missed you."

"First time I've ever heard that from one of my boys."

"Well . . . maybe I changed my mind. Maybe I don't wanna be one of your boys anymore."

She could almost hear him smiling. "You diggin' a niggah?"

Collyn laughed. She hadn't felt this giddy or this nervous since high school. "You're so arrogant."

"And you love it."

"Yeah," she said to herself more than to him, "too much of it . . ."

"So answer my question."

"Look, all I'm sayin' is that I'm here. And honestly, I can't stop thinking about you." She stopped herself; she was admitting too much. "But I mean, it's cool if you're in another space right now. After all, it has been a while since we've last seen each other."

"It's been a month," he said. "And if I was in another space, I wouldn't have answered the phone."

"I'm just making a statement. I mean, hell, you could be married."

"I'm not."

"I'm just sayin'."

"I'm just answerin'."

"I mean, you could be involved."

"Look, why you going around and around? I'm not married, I'm not involved, I'm here wanting to chill with you."

Silence.

"You know what your problem is?" he said. "You always want what you want when you want it. But it doesn't work that way. Life does what the fuck it wants to do. And all I know is that I'm here and I'm not a man who plays games, so if I wasn't true, I wouldn't have even stepped to you."

"Why haven't I heard from you?"

"That was your call."

"My call?"

"Exactly."

"So what is it now?"

"No games, no secrets."

She snuggled in her bed, the sound of his voice turned her on by the moment. "And then what?"

"And then it's just me and you." Collyn eased her hand down the middle of her thighs. His deep voice sounded like sweet honey over the phone. She imagined him lying in bed naked, with a hard dick waiting for her to melt onto it and defined abs missing her sweet kisses.

"What you thinking, love?"

"Honestly?" She was surprised at her own response. "I'm thinking about how I really wanna get to know you."

"So what's the problem?"

"This is just so different."

"What's different, beautiful? 'Cause I'm honest about how I feel about you? I'm grown, baby, thirty-four years old, and all I know how to do is be real about how I feel. So if you want me, and you want me to be with you and to please you, then you have to tell me, so I'll know exactly what to do."

Collyn closed her eyes. Chills radiated through her, making the desire for him even more intense. Desire stirred between her thighs as he continued to speak. She placed her hand over her silky mountain and played with its peak. "So if I wanted you here, tell me, what would you do?" she squeezed her clit as if she expected juice to flow from it.

"Anything you wanted me to."

"What if I wanted you to make love to me?" she asked breathlessly smearing her wet finger all over her pussy's lips.

"Then I would." His voice dropped a sexy octave.

"How would you start?"

"I'd slide wet kisses down your neck to your plump nipples. And I know they're fat because I could tell by the imprint they were big enough to fit perfectly on my tongue. Why don't you touch 'em for me?"

Collyn granted his request, tenderly grabbing her breasts and massaging her nipples.

"Now take your tongue and lick them slowly for me."

She did, making sure he could hear the gentle smacking of her lips.

"My tongue," he continued on, "wouldn't stop at your nipples. I'd lick a wet trail between your legs to your sweet drippings. Mmmm . . . slide your fingers through that juice for me." She did as he commanded. "Damn, I wish I could taste that juice. I know it's sweet. I wish I could have that juice drizzle over my lips. Is it a lot?"

"Yes."

"Damn, I wish I could drink that shit. Is it creamy?"

"Yes." She panted as she played in it, took her fingers and let the tips marinate in it.

"Damn I wanna eat that shit. Is it silky?"

"Mmm . . . yes." Her chest heaved.

"Can you feel my fingers running through your flesh like fire?"

"Mmm-hmmm." Collyn was trembling with desire. She lifted her legs to her chest in a daze.

"I want you to play with that pussy . . . you playing in that pussy for me?" he moaned.

"Mmm . . ." was the closest she could get to yes.

"You feelin' that pussy jump? That's how it's gon' jump against my tongue as I circle around that fat, bursting clit, blowing on it, and easing my fingers into your creamy slit."

Collyn moaned as she felt her liquid bomb get ready to explode. She arched her back, her stomach tightened, and her fingers moved like a cyclone between her erotic lips.

"You cummin', beautiful?"

She tried to say yes but she couldn't get her mouth to form any words, so her moaning would have to speak for her.

"Cum, baby, and put that pussy dead in my face, so I can kiss it, look at it, and tell it I ain't goin' nowhere."

Collyn's moaning was beyond control. She could feel waves crashing and thrashing in her belly until finally the bomb exploded. Collyn held the phone to her ear and whispered, "I want you here."

"Open the door. I'm already outside."

NINE

Sensual beats from Floetry's "Say Yes" swept through Collyn's apartment via the surround sound as she nervously prepared for her date with Bless. She knew exactly what she wanted, and at one in the morning there was no need to waste time getting to the point, especially since he was already outside. She'd asked him to give her a few minutes as she hurriedly dressed for the occasion: a formfitting black lace corset that catered to her full cleavage, a matching lace and satin G-string, and a set of garters that ran down her thick and toned thighs like strips of ebony water, connecting to ultrasheer black thigh-highs. She slipped on a pair of Bergini five-inch pumps, which propped up her already voluptuous ass and made her legs appear to go on for days.

Her hair hit her shoulders in an abundance of sexy waves. She dabbed Angel perfume between her breasts, behind her ears, and on each side of her inner thighs before heading into the master bath and filling the large tub with honey milk bath and red and white rose petals. She picked up the remote to the fireplace and turned it on. The flickering flames bounced off the soapstone that encased the tub.

She lit various-sized white candles and placed them strategically throughout the bath. She poured two glasses of chilled white wine, and just as she sat them on the edge of the tub, alongside strawberries, cream, and a loofah sponge, her phone rang. It was security letting her know her guest had arrived.

Suppressing the butterflies in her stomach, she walked to the door, opened it and leaned against the door frame, the illuminated view of the city created a seductive backdrop. The elevator doors opened and Bless looked directly at her, his beautiful body glowing like honey-coated chocolate. He wore simple street gear: a fitted white wife-beater, baggy jeans, and Timbs. Collyn took a deep breath. She knew at this moment that she was on her way to giving her all to him.

As he stood before her, she took his hand and welcomed him into her world.

The automatic locks clicked, and his eyes roamed her brick-house body in amazement. "Damn, beautiful." He sat on the arm of her chair and placed his hands on her waist. "Every time I see you, you get prettier." He ran his hands down the sides of her thighs, the silkiness of her stockings caressing the palms of his hands.

Collyn's body trembled as he outlined her throbbing middle with the tip of his index finger before kissing the face of her G-string and moving it to the side. He looked her dead in the eyes as he slid his tongue in, slightly blowing on her clit and then magically sucking it, causing her to cream and scream instantly. Her clit felt like Jell-O between his smooth lips as he gave her one last lick.

He stood up from the chair, placed one hand on her waist and the other behind her left thigh, and stared at her. His eyes told her a thousand times that she was beautiful. She locked her arms around his neck, and he kissed her, slowly, deeply, beyond passionately. She melted in his arms, doing all she could to catch her breath as she pressed against his hard chest.

Though they'd spoken only a few words, their embrace said so much more. Collyn took Bless by the hand and led him to the master bath. The flames of the fireplace and candles flickered against the natural stone like diamonds, while the glass ceiling and view of the city gave the essence of being on top of the world.

Slowly he undressed her, taking his time undoing the hooks and eyes of her corset, and when he was done he tossed it to the floor. He pulled at the sides of her G-string, caressing it off her. Collyn wasn't sure how or when he'd taken her thigh-highs and stilettos off, but she knew they were gone when she stood completely naked before him.

As she undressed him, she placed a Halls in her mouth and began to kiss down his chest, her tongue outlining the creases in his washboard. Afterward her mouth traveled to the center of his defined thighs, where she lovingly worked all ten inches of him into her mouth.

The menthol between her cheeks made his pre-cum run like rain, glistening her lips. She licked the length, running her wet and warm tongue against the bulging veins, sucking only the tip when she reached it. She licked and licked from the base to the tip, and then once again she swallowed him whole.

The sensual sound of her gracious mouth deep-throating him drove him wild. He didn't know if he should continue to run his fingers through her hair or to brace himself against the sides of the tub to hold himself up.

She lifted her eyes. "You like?"

Before he could respond she took him back into her mouth. Bless tried to hold on as long as he could, but as Collyn took him to the back of her throat and her tongue continued to showcase it's talents, he couldn't contain himself any longer. "Fuck ma." He eased from her mouth, picked her up, and placed her in the bath, the honey milk splashing all over her body and against the sides of the tub.

He joined her and the caramel in his skin blended into hers. His chest pressed against her breasts as the honey milk dripped from her hands and ran over his shoulders. She kissed him all over his face, his neck, his shoulders, and his chest. She licked his nipples as his wet hands pulled her hair back, causing her to look into his face. He kissed her from her lips to her succulent breasts, sucking her nipples as if he longed to be breastfed. He teased them with the tip of his tongue, rotating from one to the other.

She could feel his dick pressed against her aching clit and she couldn't wait any longer to feel him inside of her, so she massaged him until he opened her slit and eased his huge rod into the center of her wetness. Though she wasn't a virgin, she felt like one. Never had she been filled up to this degree, and just when she thought he had it all in, she felt him pushing and realized there was more. She lifted her thighs, the honey milk splashing all over the floor as she placed her legs on the side of the bath, allowing him full access to her heated sex.

They stared into each other's face, each of them wondering the same things, how he felt and how she felt, now that they'd connected, marrying their souls, their creams, their lives at least for this moment intertwined. She pulled him closer, and

her warmth seduced him to go deeper. He stroked her with all
he had, the tip, the sides, and the base of his monstrous dick,
creating wonderful friction against her G-spot, forcing her to
scream and call out his full name. "Blessing Shields . . ."

"I'm here, baby."

"Damn, it feels . . ." She stopped because she was lost for
words; there were no adjectives to describe how she felt and
how he felt inside of her.

He licked the tips of her nipples, and then he suckled once
again as if there were milk that she could give him.

"I just wanna know," Collyn whispered, "what's it like inside me . . ."

"So fuckin' wet"—he stroked—"and so fuckin' warm . . .
shhhhh—shit, I feel"—he stroked her harder—"every part of
you. It's like I know that one day I'ma look up and I'ma love
the hell outta you."

Collyn's orgasm stirred in her belly as he continued to
pound and seduce it to be released.

"The first time I saw you," Bless moaned as he stroked, "I
thought you were too fuckin' beautiful for words."

Again she kissed him all over his face, his lips, his eyes, his
chin. She didn't want him to move, yet she didn't want him to
stay still. This was the best she'd ever felt in her life.

He looked her dead in the eyes and whispered, "After I saw
you I was fucked up for a minute, because I'd abandoned
everything and all of the reasons why I was there." He stroked
her slowly yet passionately, with a tight firm grip, working her
over to no end.

She closed her eyes, her thighs trembling.

"Look at me," he said in a soft but demanding tone. "I don't
want you to run from me anymore. You understand?"

"Yes," she moaned.

He pounded her over and over, causing her to scream, "Blessssssssssing!"

"I ain't going nowhere, baby." He grabbed her hips and she arched her back. He was in so deep that she wondered if she was actually breathing. Deciding that his vigorous and unrelenting thrusts, were knocking the air from her lungs, she thought to ask him if he could give her a minute to get her breath back. Yet before she could speak it was as if he read her mind and said, "You wanted this dick, now you gettin' it. So don't ask me to stop, 'cause I'm not."

"Shit!" she screamed. "Baby, wait."

"Fuck wait." He pounded, rotating his rhythm from fast to slow and back again, the honey milk splashing against his tight ass. "All I want you to know is that I got you. As long as you straight with me, we gon' always be good." He lifted her right leg and bit her shin, and just when she started to cum, he slid down her belly and sucked every ounce of sweetness her body had to offer.

"You gon' fuck around," he said, "and I'ma risk it all for you."

TO TURN ME . . .

TEN

The early morning sun blinded Monday as Kenyatta slid the thumping head of his dick between Monday's tits, as she held them together. Her pussy dripped as the water squirting dildo they played with rotated between her pussy lips. She squinted her eyes and sucked the warm tip of Kenyatta's manhood.

Monday knew that them fucking like this early in the morning was more about guilt than anything else. Which is why she felt conflicted. Especially since he'd been acting suspicious. Whenever she would ask him questions about why he was so jumpy, his constant answer had become a wet tongue, a stiff dick, or an argument; all of which had Monday mentally exhausted. She tried not to become consumed with suspicion, but she knew underneath his desperate attempts to have a together exterior that something he was lying about was haunting him.

Her tongue curled around his dick and Monday's legs trembled. Just as she closed her eyes and called his name their private line rang.

"Damn," Kenyatta looked down at her nibbling his dick and then he said, "I gotta get this."

"What?" she opened her eyes, surprised.

"Monday, I have to get this. I've been waiting on a call since yesterday."

"But . . . Kenyatta," she whined,

"I know but this is more important." He rolled over and picked up the phone, "Kenyatta Smith." He covered the mouthpiece and said to Monday, "It's Hudson."

Monday twisted her lips, "Everything seems to be more important than me."

Kenyatta frowned, "Don't start." He pointed at Monday before grabbing the cordless receiver and heading into the bathroom.

Monday laid in bed, turning her head from one side to the next looking around the room, "This is crazy." She eased out of bed, walked over to her closet, and began choosing her clothes for today. The governor's wife was having her annual "Support AIDS Research" luncheon, and although the scandal they were wrapped in had taken away Monday's desire to attend, she knew it would only look worse if she didn't show and make a donation.

As she sorted through her clothes she heard Kenyatta's BlackBerry ringing in the distance. She continued what she was doing until she heard it ring again. She turned toward the bathroom door, not sure if Kenyatta had heard it ringing or not. But when he didn't bolt out of the bathroom and act as if it were an emergency that he answer it, curiosity weighed in and ultimately pushed her to seize the moment, "Hello?" she answered.

No response. She knew someone was there because she could hear them breathing, "Hello?"

Monday took the phone from her ear, looked at the screen, and realized the person had hung up. She looked at the caller ID and saw the name. *"Tracy?"* She pressed the button so the number could be revealed. She tapped her index finger against her bottom lip. *"Who the hell is Tracy?"*

Listening to the shower continue to run, Monday chanced a few moments more and searched Kenyatta's e-mails. Most of them were from Hudson, discussing city business. Then there was one from Taryn. Seeing Taryn's name caused Monday's heart to ache even more, so she scanned the e-mail and then continued on.

As she scrolled she found three electronic receipts for three thousand dollars each for Bazemore Art Gallery. Monday stood stunned and looked around the room as if she'd just seen a ghost.

"What . . . the . . . fuck . . . are you doing?" Kenyatta spat, breathing heavily behind her neck.

Monday jumped and the muscles in her throat tightened. She quickly pressed the off button on his phone. "I was just trying to get the shit to stop ringing."

He snatched it so hard from her hand, she stumbled a few inches out of the spot she was standing in.

"Don't touch my damn phone!" He walked over to the wardrobe, "Leave my shit alone!"

Monday sucked her teeth as her nervous heart continued to pound, "You didn't have to snatch it like that!" She flicked her hand.

"Just stop snooping through my shit." He began to dress.

"Where are you going?" Monday asked politely. She was trying to restrain herself, especially since she knew he wanted her to argue with him, because that would be just the excuse he needed to say her mouth was the real reason he was leaving.

"I got shit to do, unlike you." He snapped.

Monday swallowed, "It's Saturday."

"I have a city to run."

"I can't tell. Ever since that bullshit with Eve, the city's been running itself, so spare me."

Kenyatta ignored her and continued to dress. Monday stared at him and watched sweat form on his brow and run down the side of his face. She wondered what he was thinking about and where he was really going. She thought about asking him again, but didn't feel like the lies and the argument.

So she decided at this moment on the spot that she had to follow him. To hell with feeling fucked-up every day because she couldn't believe the shit Kenyatta had to say. She was tired of not knowing and continuing to guess what he was covering up.

"Fuck it." Monday murmured as she ran in the bathroom for a quick shower, yet when she finished and stepped out of the bathroom, he'd left.

"Damn!" She seethed as she glanced out the window. She could see Kenyatta's driver opening the door for him. She got dressed, eased her Fendi shades on, left out the servant's entrance, and pulled out of the garage in her baby blue Mercedes. As she blended into the street she was a half a block behind Kenyatta's town car. She threaded through traffic like a city cab driver, keeping a clear view of Kenyatta, who had just made a right. As she placed her signal on to turn behind him a black Lamborghini cut her off and slammed on the brakes in front of her, causing her to run directly into the back of it! "Goddamn!"

Now she knew for sure she was going to lose it. "Mother-fucker!" she hopped out of the car. The heels of her chocolate Yves Saint Laurent stilettos clapped against the hot asphalt as she stormed toward the offending driver. Her chocolate skirt, which stopped above her knee, rode her voluptuous ass, as her thighs moved in a rhythmic motion, allowing everyone watching to see that she was pissed off. Her full cleavage bounced in her teal green V-neck, which nicely hugged her D-cups.

"What the fuck is yo' problem?" she spat as the other driver stepped out of his car.

"My fault." He said as he walked to where his Lamborghini touched her Mercedes. "I don't think there's any damage, though." Slowly he squatted to his knees.

Monday sucked her bottom lip into her mouth as she noticed the bulging veins running from his large hands to his defined biceps and triceps.

His nylon wife-beater draped on his defined chest and the long basketball shorts he rocked fell on his hips just right.

Hating that her admiration of his beauty had distracted her, she snapped, "What do you mean *you don't think* there's damage! Of course there's damage, along with you adding to my fucked-up ass morning, your piece of shit scratched the hell outta my car. What the fuck? You must be fuckin' kidding me!"

"Monday," he said, standing up and facing her, "What's with the nasty mouth? You need to calm down, it was an acci-dent—"

"Monday?" she said, surprised, she took a step back and realized it was Mehki. She quickly looked him over, "You got a habit," she spat, "of runnin' into motherfuckers!"

Mehki frowned. "Look, my apologies. I just really needed to get to the mayor and I missed my exit for the mansion. I was trying—"

"Trying what? To aggravate the shit out of me?"

"Aggravate you?" Mehki said, put off. "This isn't about you."

"I'm so sick," she laughed in disbelief "of motherfuckers and their bullshit."

"Your mouth is ridiculous. Now look, I got a call when I was playing basketball—"

"Ridiculous?" Monday was taken aback.

"Yeah, ridiculous. Anyway—"

"Who the hell are you talking to? I *am* the mayor's wife! Shit, I got your damn ridiculous!"

Mehki's eyes opened wide. "Did you forget you are a lady? I've never known you to speak like this. What happened to you?"

"What-the-fuck-ever." Monday snapped as Mehki laughed. "Are you laughing at me?"

"Actually I'm surprised as hell at you."

"Do I look like I wanna laugh with you?"

He pointed to her hard nipples. "No, you look like you wanna do more than that with me."

Monday paused and took a step back.

"Look," Mehki said, "what I was trying to explain to you—"

"You weren't trying to explain shit to me!"

"Look—"

"No, you look—"

"YO!" he said sternly, with extreme bass in his voice. "Stop cuttin' me off! Now cut all that cussin' and shit out! I've had enough of it. Pull your car over to the side, so we can let the other drivers pass."

"Pull over to the side? I don't know who you think—"

"What did I just tell you to do?" Mehki gave Monday a look that told her he was serious.

Monday couldn't believe it. He may as well have just told

her to shut the fuck up, then maybe she wouldn't have been so turned on, but at this moment all of what he just said was nothing but sheer seduction to her ears.

She stood in the middle of the street for a moment, observing the backed up traffic and the rubberneckers blowing their horns and yelling for them to move on. She looked at his license plate, "Trying to tell me it's no fuckin' damage!" She mumbled to herself as she walked to her car and got in. "Think 'cause he fuckin' cute and shit."

They pulled their cars to the side of the street and traffic started flowing again. He stepped out of his car and leaned against the hood. Monday stormed over to where he was and stood in front of him. "You will pay for this!" she spat.

"Monday, it's nothing." He said, doing his all to remain calm, "And you know I wouldn't steer you wrong. And I've apologized for the inconvenience. But when did you start acting like this? This is not you."

"I didn't ask you to fuckin' read me! And I'm different now and besides you're missing the point." She crossed her arms over her breasts, rolled her eyes, and turned her head toward the oncoming traffic, "I'm just soooo sick of all y'all mother-fuckers!"

Instead of feeding her fury he slipped the cigar from behind his left ear and lit it. The smoke rose above his onyx colored eyes like a serpent's dance. The rim of his New York Yankees baseball cap was fitted like a half moon as he watched her act like a fine-ass fool. Her thick hips swaying in front of him made him unintentionally grab his dick. She would've been just right if she hadn't run off and become the mayor's wife. Her smooth lips continued to spit some of the nastiest shit he'd ever heard come from her mouth.

"The only thing saving you right now," Monday gave a sinister laugh, "is because you so fuckin' big." Inadvertently her eyes looked toward his crotch. "Otherwise I would kick . . . yo' . . . ass!"

He lifted his baseball cap and turned it around to the back. Then he held the cigar with one hand and tucked the other hand inside his waistband. He was doing his best to let Monday get all of this off her chest, especially since he realized that none of this had anything to do with him.

After a few moments of repeating the same shit Monday noticed she was the only one going off. She looked at him, "Why the hell are you so quiet?"

"Come here." He said, as the lit cigar hung from the corner of his lips, with bits of ashes flaking toward the ground and some of it floating into the wind, "We need to talk."

"I can hear from where I'm standing."

"Didn't I just say we needed to talk?, now come here."

Monday didn't know why she was listening to him, but she did as he said anyway. Now she stood directly in front of him. He grabbed her by the waist and pulled her toward him. They were now chest to chest bathing in each other's scents. He took one last pull from his cigar before flicking it into the street.

Being that she was five-five and he was six-four she had to look up at him, a view that she'd always enjoyed.

Before he spoke he stroked her hair and stared into her eyes. He could see her fighting back the tears. "When did you become like this? This isn't you. You're cussin' like crazy, acting crazy, and I don't understand it. I mean, yeah, we had an accident but you out here acting like I ran over your mama's wheelchair. Calm down, you're too lovely for this. If anything, considering that you left me with a new pinky ring, I should be angry and upset with you, but you're pissed off enough for the two of us. And maybe you missed the memo but last I checked a lady needs to act like one, and once before you had that down pat. Now whatever the mayor did to you before you left this morning you need to take up with him, but when you come at me, remember that you are a lady. Are we clear?"

Monday had become honey in his hands, sticky, wet, and with a heart that was skipping beats. She could swear he saw her mind envisioning his dick size. She took her index finger and traced the tattoo on the right side of his arm that read *Mehki*.

Mehki looked down at Monday's full breasts and remembered slipping her hard nipples into his mouth. He lifted her face and admired her eyes, which sparkled against the morning sun rays. She was beautiful in every sense of the word. He tilted his head to the side and read her eyes, which told him that she had as much on her mind as he did, "What are you thinking?" he asked, doing his all not to kiss her.

She knew he was studying her lips as she spoke, "You go first."

"I was thinking," he paused, "if I wanted to kiss you . . . or make love to you. But I can't make up my mind."

Monday nervously swallowed as she stepped out of his embrace. "Listen," she said, "I need to go. I have someplace I need to be."

"All right." He smiled. "Here," he reached in his back pocket and pulled out a card. "Use it." He boldly took the card, reached behind her and slid it in the rear pocket of her skirt.

As he turned to leave he winked and Monday watched him get in his car. His business card felt like a seductive chill as she slid into her Mercedes and pulled off.

ELEVEN

"Collyn Bazemore, please," a tall, lean black man wearing a pair of blue Dockers and a white polo shirt said to Taryn. He took one of the gallery's business cards and placed it in his beige trench coat pocket while his partner browsed, looking at the art and raising his eyebrows at the prices.

"Do you have an appointment?" Taryn asked, knowing that he didn't.

"No," the man answered, "but I'm sure she'll see me."

"And you are?"

"Agent West." He flashed his silver badge. "FBI, Missing Persons."

Taryn blinked. "One moment, please."

"Thank you."

"Pierre," Taryn called to the art assistant who was helping a customer on the floor. He turned to look at her. "I have to run in the back for a moment." Taryn hustled to Collyn's office. She knocked and entered immediately. "Excuse me, but there are two men here to see you."

Collyn looked surprised, "Taryn," she said politely but sternly, pointing to one of her clients, "you can see I'm already with someone."

"Collyn, you don't understand." Taryn shook her head. "I really think you should take this meeting."

Collyn looked at her client, who was sitting in her chocolate leather wing chair. "Just a moment, please." She stepped out into the hallway, "Taryn, this is nothing like you. What is the problem?"

"There are two FBI agents here to see you. Missing Persons Squad."

Collyn's heart dropped. It was obvious that Kenyatta had followed through on his threat and sold the feds some bullshit.

"It's fine," Collyn said, maintaining her composure. "Show them to the clients' lounge and have Pierre serve them Moët."

Collyn walked back into her office. "Mr. Borne, it's been my pleasure. Your fantasy has been arranged. Janelle will meet you at the hotel in D.C. tomorrow by three."

"Thank you." He smiled.

"Anytime." She walked him to the back door; his limo pulled around, and he left. Afterward Collyn sauntered into the lounge, her rust-colored wrap dress blending in with the early autumn leaves sweeping the ground as she stood directly in front of the wall of windows. "Gentlemen." She held out her hand, her onyx and white-diamond tennis bracelet shimmering in the sunlight.

Both agents accepted her gesture, greeting her with lustful looks and smiles.

"What can I do for you?" She poured herself a glass of Moët and sipped.

"You have a beautiful place here," Agent West commented.

Collyn smiled. "I don't do small talk." She tried to remain calm, not wanting them to know they'd caught her off guard.

"Ms. Bazemore, I'm Agent West and this is Agent Jones. We need to ask you some questions."

"I'm listening."

"Do you know Eve Johnson?" Agent West pulled a photograph of the woman from his pocket and handed it to Collyn.

Collyn pushed back her shoulder-length curls as she looked at the picture. "Not off the top of my head." She handed the photo back to the agent.

"Look at it carefully." He shoved it back toward her face. "Because I believe you do."

"Her cell phone records indicate that she spoke to you daily," Agent Jones put in.

"Spoke to me?" Collyn smirked as she sipped her drink, her lipstick making an imprint on the glass. "Really?"

"Also," Agent Jones continued, "there were a stack of receipts found in her apartment from your gallery, totaling well into the tens of thousands of dollars."

"And I'm certain you would remember," Agent West added, "someone who purchased such large quantities of art from you."

"Agents," Collyn said with ease, "surely you didn't come here to describe a lover of art to me? People buy art from me all over the world. As a matter of fact, people commission me to find them one-of-a-kind pieces. So do you think I should remember someone specifically named Eve Johnson? Do you know how many Johnsons there are?"

"But this one called here daily," Agent West snapped.

"And so do a lot of other people," Collyn responded.

Agent Jones grimaced and waved the picture in her face. "She disappeared a little over two months ago."

"Then why aren't you looking for her?"

"We are."

"Not in here you aren't."

"We think you know her," Agent West stated again.

Sensing that they had no real evidence, Collyn looked at him as if he were silly.

"Listen." Agent West pulled up a chair. "Why don't you just tell us what happened? Perhaps if you tell us the truth, then we can talk to the prosecutor and see about cutting you a deal."

Collyn forced herself not to flip. "Cut me a deal?" She all but laughed in his face. "Are you charging me with something?"

"Listen—"

"I'm not listening to shit anymore," she said.

"Okay, you wanna play that game?" Agent Jones growled. "How about this: I have five people who say you know exactly who Eve Johnson is. Those same people also said you argued with her over money and that the next day, the very next day after your argument, she was missing. Coincidence? I don't think so. Now, why don't you tell us what really happened?"

Collyn clapped her hands. "Agents, it sounds to me like you have a beautiful case sewn up, especially with five people who all seem to know exactly what happened. So I don't see what you need my statement for. Charge me with whatever they said I did and get the shit over with."

When they didn't respond, she continued, "That's what I thought. Now, let me explain something to you. This is an art gallery, and unless you came to purchase some of my pieces, get out and don't come back, do you understand?"

The agents glared at her. They had no charges and the theory they presented was bogus, so they couldn't go anywhere with that. All they had was a daily log of cell phone calls and a ton of receipts for art. "Funny thing is," Agent West said, "there were a lot of receipts for art, but we didn't find any art in Eve's apartment."

"Have a good day, Ms. Bazemore," Agent Jones said as they nodded and left.

Collyn simmered as she watched them get into their gray Crown Victoria and leave. Once they'd disappeared down the busy street, Collyn turned to Taryn. "I'll be back. I gotta motherfucker I need to see."

Twenty minutes later, after ducking and dodging through traffic, Collyn was at City Hall. She went through the metal detector, signed in, and caught the elevator to the floor where the mayor's office was. Collyn didn't wait for Kenyatta's secretary to call him on the intercom, instead she stormed passed her, flung the door wide open, and slammed it behind her.

There were scrambling noises as she walked in and sat down in the burgundy Queen Anne chair facing him. She crossed her thick thighs and her purse made a loud thud as she threw it onto Kenyatta's desk. "Okay, motherfucker." Collyn tapped the pencil heel of her stiletto on the eagle's face woven into the blue carpet. "What the fuck was sending the feds to my office about?"

Kenyatta cleared his throat. It was obvious that he had been caught off guard. Collyn was the last person he expected to see, especially since he was in the midst of taking care of some personal business. "What are you doing here? I didn't send any feds to your office. And I'm busy." He waved security away as they rushed into his doorway.

Collyn stood up and leaned over his heavy mahogany desk. A pair of brown kitten heels protruded from under the desk on her side. "Do you think I give a fuck about that bitch suckin' yo' li'l-ass dick under your desk? Do you think I give a good goddamn?" She kicked the woman's shoes. There was a thump under the desk.

"Pathetic . . ." She shook her head. "Consider this a promise: if you gon' fuck with me, then you better come wit' it, because I'm not playing games with you. Let another goddamn cop, agent, who-the-fuck-ever come to my place of business, get in my face again, and see if I don't regulate everybody up in this motherfucker. Won't nobody in this bitch have a political career!"

"Wait a minute now—"

"I don't have another minute to wait for your ass. So my suggestion to you"—she pursed her lips—"is to take heed to what the fuck I just said. Be clear, I am not the one you need to fuck with." She grabbed her purse and stormed out of his office, brushing the security guard, who was standing outside of the doorway, on the shoulder.

By the time she arrived back at the gallery, she exceeded furious. "Where is Taryn?" she snapped at Pierre.

"She had to leave for a moment. The sitter called and said the baby was sick. But Collyn," he said as if he were in a hurry, "the mayor's—"

Before he could finish, Monday stood up. "I got a problem with you, and you will speak to me right now!"

Collyn took a step back. She hadn't seen Monday in years, and looking in her face today, the reunion was too soon. She looked Monday over, noticed that not much had changed, and said slowly, "What . . . the . . . fuck . . . do you want?" Suddenly the entire gallery became quiet and all the customers froze in their spots.

Finally remembering where she was, Collyn smiled and said to Monday, "Follow me please."

Their heels clicked in an angry rhythm as they stormed toward Collyn's office.

Once they reached the office Collyn slammed the door, then turned on the TV to drown out the argument that was about to ensue.

"How fuckin' dare you service my husband!" Monday screamed. I moved away from you, but I swear to God, everywhere I go, there you are. I've been through enough shit in my last life and I don't need you reincarnating the same goddamn drama in this one!"

"What—" Collyn scrunched up her face and looked at Monday as if she had two heads, "Excuse me?"

"I'm not finished," Monday said, enraged. "All this time I've been thinking that I was dealing with an average everyday bitch and it's one of your hoes! Make no mistake, if you send Tracy or whatever other bitch again—"

"Tracy?" Collyn said, put off. "What are you talking about?"

"You know what I'm talking about!" Monday balled her fist and slammed it on Collyn's desk, rattling the phone and the penholder, causing the holder to topple over and fall to the floor. "Don't even attempt to lie, because I found the dummy receipts from your gallery in his e-mail. You must think my life is a game that I'm playin'. Leave my fuckin' husband alone!"

"Your goddamn husband—"

"Is none of your concern."

"It is when it's affecting my business."

"If you didn't have some bottom bitch named Tracy fucking him—"

"Who the hell is Tracy?" Collyn screamed. "Kenyatta's bottom bitch was named Eve," she spat coldly.

"Eve?" Monday said, filled with air.

Monday took a step back and Collyn spat, "Don't you ever bring yo' ass up in here like this again! Perhaps I need to remind you of just who the fuck I am." Collyn got in Monday's face, squinted her eyes, and said in a sinister whisper, "I am your pimp, bitch." She pointed into Monday's face. "Once a ho always a ho. You met that niggah because of me and my dough. You were on my payroll—or did you actually start to believe that made-up bullshit you tell the press? Did you forget that sucking dick paid your way through law school?"

Silence.

"Oh yeah, baby, it's me, superbitch. I'm Godmama," Collyn pointed to her chest, "and don't you ever in your life forget that shit!"

"I didn't forget! But I chose a different life."

"Well, you didn't run far enough!"

"I don't want to keep being haunted by this shit! That's why I came to New York. That's why I worked so hard for my life to be different. I have no one, except my husband, and I never expected to see you again. I thought that part of my life was over when I left Atlanta, only for me to wake up one morning and find you here."

"What? What the hell, are you, nuts? I was born and raised in New York, I don't have to run from you, that's your m.o."

"Then why are you in my fuckin' life again?"

"You came to see me. I didn't seek you out!"

"What did you expect? You're servicing my husband with some bitch named Tracy, and here I am trying to be a good wife. And I worked too hard to have to contend with this bullshit."

Collyn looked at Monday, taken aback, "Geneva Thompson, just 'cause you changed your name to Monday Clark, doesn't mean you changed who you are. Underneath all that political husband and wife bullshit is a ho and a trick. And if you think it's any different, then you need to look again.

"Now I don't know who the fuck Tracy is, but she ain't here, the last time that motherfucker bought some pussy from me, it was from Eve."

"Are you—"

"I'm not finished! Now you need to be clear, that niggah doesn't give a damn about anything other than himself, and the quicker you get with the program the better off you will be."

Suddenly Monday felt as if the wind had been knocked out of her. Tears streamed down her cheeks as she looked around Collyn's office in despair.

Geneva had been poor. From the outskirts of Atlanta, she'd been on her own since she was seventeen. She never knew her real mother, who'd been too busy chasing the demons of possessed dick to be bothered with raising a child. So her father raised her, at least until he remarried and announced to her at seventeen that she was grown and needed to make it on her own. And outside of a city welfare grant and a scholarship, all she had left were her dreams.

She met Collyn in college, they weren't best friends, but they were cordial. At the time Collyn ran an elite escort service and Monday found herself in a predicament where she needed cash, so she did what she had to do. The only problem now was that she needed to have that part of her life buried, especially since Kenyatta didn't know about it.

Collyn sighed. She knew Monday's life was much different from hers. Collyn had grown up hood rich with a mother who handed her a family business, and all Monday had was the here and now. Collyn blew air from the side of her mouth, "Look, I don't know what you want from me."

"All I want is someone who will tell me the truth. What the hell is really going on?"

"I just told you the truth!"

"No," Monday shook her head, "I can't believe that he

would lie to that extent. Why? Why would he lie about knowing her." Monday said, distantly speaking more to herself than to Collyn.

"Monday," Collyn said, "I've always been honest with you. Always. Now if you want me to tell you the truth, then you have to tell me what you're talking about, because right now my nerves can't take this guessing shit. He lied about knowing who?"

"Eve. He said he only saw her once and could barely remember what she looked like."

Collyn paused. Kenyatta never ceased to amaze her. "That's a lie, he fucked Eve quite a few times."

Monday was silent and tears streamed from her eyes.

"Please don't cry," Collyn said, "because I can't do the emotional thing right now. You gon' have to swallow that shit. Now I understand that you're trying to be normal, political, or whatever but you have to look at this for what it is. Because you cannot make everything ugly that he does go away." She handed Monday a tissue.

"I know," she wiped the tears from her eyes, "I know and it hasn't been easy. I mean I would've never found out you were here if it hadn't have been for Kenyatta's affair with Taryn. I hate to even think about that shit. That really messed me up."

"Yeah, it messed you up to the point where he doesn't even acknowledge his daughter."

"Yes, he does," Monday snapped. "He sneaks to see her."

"What? Taryn didn't tell me that."

"She e-mailed him. I found it when I was trying to find out who Tracy was. I don't want to talk about Taryn though. I just want to know who this person, Tracy, is. She called this morning and hung up."

"Do you remember the number?"

"No, only the first three digits."

"Damn, well I can't help you with the Tracy shit."
Monday looked around the room in despair.

"So what now?" Collyn asked.

"I don't know. I mean, you're telling me things I didn't even know existed."

"You didn't know or you didn't want to face it."

Monday's silence answered for her.

"If it helps any," Collyn said, "I'm just as confused as you."

"Do you know where Eve is?" Monday asked.

"No, she just disappeared, she was supposed to have been on assignment, but she never showed up there."

"When was the last time," Monday swallowed, "she was with Kenyatta?"

"July Fourth weekend."

"July Fourth?"

"Yes, but I'm not sure if I believe it. I think he saw her after that. Especially since he came to see me shortly after she disappeared as if he was coming to see if I shot the bitch or some shit."

"July Fourth?" Monday stared off into space. Thinking back to how she waited for him that night and he never came home. "That's the night." She murmured.

"Night of what?"

"Nothing."

"Nothing?" Collyn looked at her suspiciously. "Okay . . . so what are you going to do from here, Monday?"

"I don't know," Tears formed in Monday's eyes again. "I don't know."

"Well I do. You gon' brush your shoulders off," she handed her another tissue to wipe her eyes, "go home, get your shit together, and watch that niggah. Trust me, he ain't that slick and his ass has slipped up somewhere. Now I don't know what he's up to, but I feel like he has something to do with Eve and her disappearance."

Monday felt conflicted, she knew Kenyatta was sneaky and capable of many things, but she wasn't sure if Eve's disappearance was one of them. "Maybe . . ." she sighed, "I just . . . I just feel lost . . ."

"Look," Collyn placed her hand on Monday's shoulder, "I know our past isn't that pleasant, but if you need me I'm here."

"Thank you." Monday managed a smile.

"But, if you ever," Collyn stood back and looked through her, "run up in here with some bullshit, I'ma lay me out a bitch."

Monday laughed, "You always talking about you gon' lay you out a bitch and you ain't shot nobody yet. Shut up."

Both of the women laughed, yet both of them knew that nothing was really funny.

"Now, look," Collyn said as if she were exhausted, "I've had a fucked-up day and I'm getting ready to leave and stop by the liquor sto'," she said in a playful Ebonics dialect, "go home and get my buzz on."

"All right," Monday said, "drink enough for both of us."

TWELVE

Rain fell from the late September sky and the glow from
the Empire State Building reflected off the low clouds as
Collyn lay in the center of her king-sized bed, staring at
her panoramic view of the New York City skyline. Never
had such an exquisite sight made her feel as lonely as she
did tonight. She wanted to relax her pride, at least for a
moment, so she could call Bless and see if he would come
over. She wasn't playing games or trying to lead him on
a cat-and-mouse chase, but she couldn't decipher the fine
line of sweatin' him versus simply wanting to see him.
Besides, she didn't want it to seem as if all of a sudden it
was all about him. But fuck it, somehow at this moment,
as her mind replayed their night of wondrous passion and

her index finger stroked tears from her aching clit, it *was* all about him.

As the rain pounded against the skylights in her ceiling her phone rang. "Hello?"

"Ms. Bazemore, this is Adam from the lobby. You have a Mr. Shields here to see you. A Mr. Bless Shields."

Immediately Collyn lost her breath. Her heart raced, and she couldn't stop smiling. Suddenly nervous, she scanned the room to see if anything was out of place. "Yes, Adam, send him up, please. Thank you."

Collyn hopped up from the bed, and before she could decide if she wanted to change out of her Juicy Couture powder-pink terry-cloth short-shorts and fitted tee, her doorbell rang. She walked to the door and opened it.

Bless leaned against the door frame and his smile lit up the hallway. "What? You ain't beat for a niggah?"

He was so fuckin' cute it didn't make sense. Collyn ran her index finger down the indent between his protruding pecs, stopping at one of his belt loops. "Who told you that?"

"You did when you didn't call me." He gave her a light kiss.

"You didn't call me either." She kissed him back.

"Beautiful, I don't call; I just show up. I came to case out the place and see if you got another niggah in here that requires me and my nine to pay him some attention."

She laughed. "Oh, what you packin'?"

"You tell me."

Pressing her lips against his, she said, "Oh, you packin', baby."

Bless laughed and tapped Collyn on the behind as she turned to go into the apartment. He picked up a plastic bag, which he'd sat on the floor when he rang the bell, and walked in behind her.

"What's in the bag?" she asked as he placed it on her kitchen island and she hopped on the bar stool.

"I brought you something to eat, so I hope you like Chinese." He removed cartons, chopsticks, and two chilled Guinness Stouts. "Figured you needed to relax for a minute." He twisted the top off her beer. "I mean . . . unless you don't drink beer."

"Would you give me my drink and stop playing with me?" She took a sip. "So what's with the food? You think I can't cook?"

Bless didn't answer. He simply smiled and handed her a set of chopsticks and soy sauce. "Here." He pointed to her carton. "Hook that up."

"Oh, you trying to be funny?" She opened the carton of shrimp lo mein and poured in the soy sauce.

"Nah, beautiful, it's your world." He started eating his lobster lo mein.

"I'll have you know that I can cook." She wiggled her neck.

"Yo, I believe you." He playfully twisted his lips in disbelief. "My baby can cook her ass off."

She blushed. She liked the sound of being called "my baby." "I can show you better than I can tell you." She looked at him and wrinkled her nose. "Punk."

He leaned over the island and into her face, "Aw, my baby mad?"

There it was again.

"But check it," he continued, "I don't know if you can cook, but you damn sure taste good."

"You are so nasty."

"I sure am." He lined kisses up her collarbone and to her chin.

Chills ran through Collyn's body. As she tried to shake the shiver off, she grabbed the plastic bag and looked inside. "How you come up in here without an egg roll, man?"

"My fault, love, but I can hook you up with some purple haze and some grape Kool-Aid."

"Fuck the haze, but I want my goddamn Kool-Aid." She playfully smirked. "And put a whole bag of sugar in it too."

"I got the sugar beat." He fed her from his chopsticks.

"What?" Collyn said, catching a noodle slipping from her lips. "What you put in your Kool-Aid?"

"Aunt Jemima syrup."

"Aunt Jemima who?" she asked in shock.

"Butter light. Do *not* get it twisted. Me and my sisters use to house us some grape Kool-Aid mixed with Aunt Jemima syrup."

"I'm in a diabetic coma just listening to that."

Collyn and Bless finished up their food and laughed and chatted for hours as they talked about everything under the sun, from the things they liked to do as kids to some of the silly shit they still did. "Now wait a minute, Bless," Collyn snickered. "What exactly do you mean, you used to rap?" She arched her eyebrows as they sat on the sectional. "Like you used to make beats and shit?"

"Hell yeah, and I was the fresh too. I should've pursued that. I'm thinking about going back." He nodded in assurance.

Collyn couldn't tell if he was serious or not, yet she hoped like hell that he wasn't because she was only seconds away from laughing in his face. "Really? So what, you sit down and make up rhymes?"

"You tryna be funny?"

"Nah, baby, do you? Women will probably trip over yo' fine-ass rappin'." She turned her head away from him and laughter eased out the side of her lips.

"You laughing at me?" he said.

"Laughing? Oh no, baby. I'm with you. As a matter of fact, I think you should call yourself Fifty-five Cent." Not able to hold it in any longer, she fell out laughing. "I'm sorry, Bless, I am."

"I got your sorry!" He tickled her, and she ended up holding on to his arms with her head lying in his lap.

Collyn was out of breath. "Okay, I'm sorry."

"No, you're not."

"I am, and I wanna hear you rap."

"Fa' real?"

"Yeah, baby, I sure do."

"Ai'ight, bust it." He rhymed, "I left my wallet in El Segundo and I wanna put my pick inside your Afro."

Collyn sat up and looked at him with a straight face, "Tell me you didn't say that." She got off the couch.

"What?" He followed her.

"Don't rap anymore. Leave that for the professionals."

"So, what exactly are you trying to say?" He stood behind her as she opened the hall closet and took out a game.

Bless looked at Collyn like she was crazy. "What the fuck is that?"

"A game."

"I see. And what you gon' do with that?"

"I wanna play."

"Oh, ai'ight, you can play, but I'm too damn big and grown to be playing a kids' game. Nah, not me." He read the box. "And then you expect me to play Twister? Do you see me? I'ma grown-ass man, dawg, I'm not 'bout to be spinning around and shit. Nah, you got Blessing Shields, fucked up."

Collyn placed her hands on her hips. "You just sat up here and rapped the corniest shit in the world to me and you too thugged out to play a game? Please. Plus"—she whined just a bit to soften him—"it'll be fun." She gave him an innocent smile.

"Don't look at me like that," Bless said, giving in, "'cause ain't shit innocent about you. Come on and don't tell nobody my big ass was up in here playing no damn kids' game either."

Collyn snickered as she set up the game, spreading the polka-dot mat on the floor. "Okay, I'll call body parts and you call colors."

"Straight." He lifted his shirt off, revealing his glued-tight wife-beater. The muscles in his arms flexed with every word he said. "If we gon' play this shit, we gon' do it different than I did when I played my sisters."

"I thought you'd never played."

"I never said that. When I was a kid, I use to bust my sisters' asses, especially since I was taller than them. Man, please. But since I'm fucking you—"

"Damn, can you be any more crude than that?"

"You know how I do it." He laughed. "So here are the rules: no clothes and baby oil."

"You smokin' haze?"

"No, why? You got some?" He gave her half a grin. "I ain't had no weed in years."

"No," she said with a frown, "I don't have any."

"Damn, 'cause I was 'bout to say light it up. Now come on, don't be trying to stall. Go get some baby oil and take them clothes off."

"And where is the oil going?"

"On the mat." He smacked her on the ass. "Come on now."

Reluctantly Collyn went into the bathroom, grabbed the baby oil, and came back. She walked over to Bless and un-buckled his pants. Pulling his belt through the loops, she said, "You know I'ma win, don't you?"

"Whatever." He stepped out of his pants, revealing his box-ers and the muscles running down his chocolate legs.

Collyn lifted her shirt over her head and stepped out of her shorts, revealing a red lace bra and thong. "Look at you." Bless licked his lips. "Fuck taking the clothes off. I need you walking around in that for a minute."

"And don't touch me either," Collyn said.

"Shit, you may as well call it quits, 'cause my ass is about to cheat." Bless squirted a little baby oil on the mat. "Madam, you may go first."

"I bet. Okay, left foot." She stepped on the mat and slipped just a little.

"Oh, don't bust ya ass, 'cause if you fall, you automatically lose. Now, yellow right corner circle."

Collyn stepped on the circle. Doing what she could to hold her balance, she said, "Ai'ight, your turn. Right hand."

"Left red circle." He grinned. "The one right there."

"Blessing, that's between my legs."

"Exactly." He reached down toward the circle between her legs, his face directly facing her vagina. She looked down at him and he started fingering her panties, "Would you stop?"

"Damn, this shit fat." He pulled the crotch of her panties back and licked her clit.

She felt her legs starting to tremble. "You cheatin'."

"I told you I was gon' cheat." He smiled. "Go 'head, call another body part."

Collyn sucked her teeth, although she was enjoying the heat radiating between her thighs. "Right foot."

"Green circle."

Collyn turned around, and Bless pointed. "That motherfucker right there."

"Oh no, yo' ass didn't." She looked at the circle, which was between his legs. "You are such a cheater."

"Nah, beautiful, it's called kama sutra. You of all people should know that."

"No, yo' ass is kama nasty."

"Call it what you want, but you better touch that damn circle."

"Ai'ight." Collyn twisted around and almost fell trying to keep her hand on the yellow circle while she put her right foot on the green one. She did what she could to maintain her balance, but since standing up proved to be a struggle, she sat down—directly on Bless' hard dick, causing him to fall flat to the floor.

"I don't believe you put all that ass on my dick like that."

"Oh, you don't want this?" She leaned forward on all fours, threw her ass in the air, and started smacking her cheeks. "Now I pick your left hand—"

"Fuck the left hand," he said, "you better pick this dick." She could feel him rubbing the head against her ass.

"You don't wanna play anymore?"

"Yeah, but now I wanna play a different game."

Collyn turned around to face him and stuck her index finger suggestively in her mouth. "Oh, you missed this sweetness?" She slid her thong off, tossed it across the room, then took her thumbs and showcased her heated pearl, the face of it radiating with sweet glaze.

"The question is, did it miss me—or better yet, did you?"

"Yes."

"Which one?"

"Both."

He stroked his hard and luscious dick. Instantly her mouth started to water as her heart traveled to between her legs and her clit thumped against her fingertip. The midnight view of the city lights cast red waves across his sugar-daddy body. Collyn pushed tears of pleasure that danced in her throat to the side as she envisioned Bless' body on top of her, pumping, thrusting, and causing her to tremble.

The longer she stared at his luscious pipe the more her breathing stifled and the warmth from her pussy made creamy liquid between her thighs. She ran her tongue across her fingertips before turning her palms up, causing him to halt in his spot.

With the grace of a panther she glided toward him, her hair sweeping her shoulders. Once she was before him, she made a wet trail with her tongue up his thighs, where she licked between his muscle creases, the sweet salt from his skin melting in her mouth.

Bless moaned softly as she outlined his shaft with soft bites and succulent kisses before taking him into her mouth and seducing the tip of his dick to the back of her throat.

Bless' moans grew louder as he fought like hell to keep his eyes open. Collyn slipped his dick out of her mouth and licked the sides of the head. Bless bit his bottom lip. A head job like this is what sent you to the moon and left you there.

He knew he would have a hangover when Collyn's tongue was done. "I swear to God," he breathed, squeezing his lips tight, water lining his eyelids, "you better not ever fuck with nobody else."

She didn't answer. Instead she continued to lick.

"I'm not fuckin' playin'." Bless' knees shook. He couldn't take it anymore. "Goddamn," was all he could say as he took his hands and ran them up and down her back. Her lips made classical music as his erotic liquid eased to the tip. "Shit . . ." He ran his hands through her hair. "Damn . . ." He gripped it. "Motherfucker . . ." He cupped her chin, and she stopped long enough to bite his fingers, then resumed sucking him.

"Tell me." She licked the length of it. "How many licks does it take to get to the center of a Toostie Roll Pop?" She swallowed him whole again.

Unable to speak and totally caught off guard, Bless stretched his long arms across Collyn's curled back and eased his warm pearls down her throat.

The moment he pulled from between her lips he became hard again; the sight of it was the prettiest thing Collyn had ever seen. She lay back on the floor and opened her legs like scissors. "Come and fulfill your fantasy, baby. Anything you've ever dreamed of is right here." She showcased every ounce of her pink river.

Bless lifted her legs from the floor and placed her in the wheelbarrow position, and she locked her ankles behind his back. He coated his dick in her wetness and then eased into her warm flesh, while taking his hands and caressing her hips. He stroked and instantly she screamed, "Jeeeeeeeee'susssssss . . ." He soared into her, her mouth flying open with every stroke. "Bless . . . !"

He pounded her harder than ever before, the swift motions of his hips causing his scrotum to slap against her ass. She knew when he was done it would be impossible to walk; this was fucking, loving, and lusting at its finest.

Collyn's orgasm took over her body, and she screamed so loud, the windows howled. She felt a series of cold chills. She started to shake as orgasmic waves crashed from between her legs.

Bless took out his dick, saw how her cream had drowned it, and said, "Look at this shit." He entered her again and within a matter of minutes he was exploding into her flesh.

He collapsed onto her and kissed her all over her face. "Damn, beautiful—" He was interrupted by his phone ringing. He rolled over the oily mat, reached for his jeans, and pulled his phone from his side pocket.

He stared at the caller ID a moment too long before answering his phone. "Bless Shields."

Although Collyn hated that she could hear a woman's voice,

she hated even more that she cared. She watched his defined back as he sat up and spoke into the phone. "No," he said matter-of-factly, "I wasn't aware of that . . . Yes . . . yes." He turned and looked at Collyn. "Right now?"

Collyn's eyes lowered, and he cupped her chin and kissed her. "All right, no problem." He hung up. "Baby—"

"Look," she sighed, "don't start explaining. It's cool. This is all in fun, right? We chillin'."

"Chillin'?"

"We cool."

"You startin' that bullshit again?" He frowned. "Look, let me just clear this up. That was my assistant, Pamela. She helps me manage my office buildings. She's also over the waterfront project I just accepted from Kenyatta. So don't trip because you heard her voice."

"Trip? Please." She swallowed. "I'm not the type. I mean, look, it is what it is. No demands, no expectations. Right?"

"Ai'ight, you 'bout to be left sittin' here again, so let me dead this shit. I like you. I more than like you; I want you. And I'm not going through this every time you feel insecure about something. I don't know who scared you, who hurt you, or what they did, but I'm not them. So let's put some definition to this shit. You want me to be your man? Scratch that: I wanna be your man. Would you like that?"

"Bless—"

"Answer me."

"Bless—"

"Tell me." He placed his index finger against her lips. "In one word."

Within seconds Collyn's inhibitions and fears of love flashed before her and caused her stomach to do flips. Though her mind was hesitant, her heart knew exactly what it wanted. "Yes."

"Straight. Then accept the fact that I'm here. I'm here with you." He looked her dead in the eyes. "And the way I feel right now, it could never be about anybody else. Now, I need to run for a minute, but I'll be back." He picked his clothes up off the floor. "All right?"

She nodded as he headed into the bathroom for a quick shower. He kissed her before he left, and Collyn watched the door close behind him. She listened to the automatic locks click into the frame as she lay back on the floor, his scent lingering in the room, and she wondered if all of this was the makings of being caught up.

**FROM A WOMAN
OF SUBSTANCE . . .**

THIRTEEN

Her pussy creamed as she sat at her bay window, sipping a glass of white wine and watching him park his Jag on the far corner. Her heart raced and her nipples hardened as she remembered it had been close to four months since he'd started to come by without calling. At most he would drop money off for the baby and be on his way, especially since the situation with Eve and his paranoia had taken over.

For a fleeting moment she thought about pretending to be busy or telling him he couldn't come in. Yet her undying desire to have him would never allow her to pretend that her obsession had been thrown to the wind.

She watched his security team park at the far end of the block while he walked around to the back of her house and turned his key in the lock. She stood in the hallway, and as he stepped in, she pushed the spaghetti straps of her lace gown down her coffee-colored shoulders and let it slither to the floor.

Immediately Kenyatta's dick hardened as he watched her beautiful body glisten in the strips of moonlight. "Don't ask me where I've been." He undid his platinum cufflinks and laid them on her counter. Slowly he undid his sky-blue button-down and pulled it from the waist of his baggy cuffed dress pants. "And I don't wanna hear no sad shit." He gradually peeled his shirt off, revealing one beautiful inch of his defined chest at a time. "And after today we can't keep going on like this. I got too many people watching me to be doing this." As he spoke, his muscular pecs came alive.

"Oh, you won't miss me? You mean to tell me that Monday will be enough to fulfill your needs? We're a family, and what is she?"

"My wife."

Regrettable tears danced in her throat as she realized she'd fallen in love with sweet air, a feel-good dream, a piece of beautiful nothing. She'd fallen in love with stolen moments, only to have to relinquish them and live on memories.

"Shhh." She grabbed his hand and led him to the kitchen chair. The sight of his beautiful body and luscious hardness made a river form between her thighs. "I'ma miss that big dick." She fell to her knees and took him into her mouth.

Kenyatta threw his head back and ran his hand through her hair. "Lick my dick right there, baby." He slipped it out of her mouth and pointed to the side of the mushroom-shaped head. "Right there." She stuck her tongue out and licked him as if his dick were melting fudge. She ran her tongue along the veins and around the head, easing her mouth under his manhood and sucking only his scrotum.

Kenyatta squeezed the muscles of his inner thighs as her jaws locked around his shaft and his knees began to shake. He couldn't take it anymore. "Goddamn" was the only sound he could make as he took his hands and placed them at the back of her neck. Her lips made love to his dick as his sweet liquid took her mouth and baptized it.

Rising from her knees, she straddled him and said, "What I'ma do without you?"

"You tell me," he said as his cock traveled into her wetness. Her thighs slapped against his as she folded her fingers together behind his neck.

"You know I'm not gon' wait forever."

"Just don't have my daughter around another man."

"Nobody even knows she's yours."

"And that's how we have to keep it."

"I thought you loved me."

"I love this pussy." He looked into her face, and she bent her neck down and bit into his bottom lip, drawing blood.

He pushed her roughly by the shoulders. "Why did you do that shit?" He glared at her. "Oh, you wanna play like that?" He yanked her hair, causing her neck to jerk back. He picked her up and carried her to the sink, where he turned the hot water on.

For a moment she was stunned, and tears raced to her eyes. She did all she could to hold them at bay as her mind tripped back to how she'd felt sitting in the closet. The hot water and the steam rose behind them. Scalding specks splashed against her ass and made her wonder if this was what Eve had felt like.

Kenyatta roughly spread her legs and entered her. He grabbed her hair and looked into her eyes. "Tell me you love this dick." He stroked with all his might.

Her ass rose off the sink as his balls slapped against her pussy lips. "I can't," she said in a breathy and seductive whisper. "You haven't given me a reason why I should love it yet."

Kenyatta stopped midstroke, and for a moment he looked at her and saw Eve. "You my bitch?"

"Hell no!" Her hips pushed against his stroke. "I'm nobody's bitch!"

Kenyatta stared back into her face, and his vision of Eve faded. "Oh, you ain't my bitch?" He bit the side of her neck, then lifted her legs in the air, causing a portion of her ass to dip into the hot water. "You ain't my bitch?"

Surprisingly, the hot water turned her on. She pulled at her nipples, and he bent down and bit them. "Ahhh," she screamed.

"Say it!" He rammed his hard dick. "Say that shit, or this'll be the last time you get this dick. Say that shit!" He bit her on the side of the neck again. "I swear to God I'll stop fucking you!" He gave her a hard thrust before he stopped his stroke and pulled out. "If you want this dick, you'll say that shit."

Her mind struggled with calling herself someone's bitch, but the mere thought of being without him and never feeling his love again caused her to trip. "No, I'm not your bitch," she whispered. "I'm your bottom bitch."

He pushed his dick back in and started stroking her with everything he had. "And don't you ever forget it! Now say it again!"

"I'm your bottom bitch!"

"No, scream that shit!"

"I'm your bottom bitch!"

"Say it again! And say it louder!"

"I'm your bottom bitch!"

"Louder!"

"I'm your bottom bitch!"

"That's what the fuck I thought," he said as his hardness

slammed so deep into her middle that she could've sworn her chest collapsed. "Don't be fuckin' playin' with me. If I tell you to fuckin' crawl, you better do that shit." He pounded and the hot water continued to rise. She could tell by looking into his face that at any moment he was going to ask her again. "You love this dick?" She mouthed it with him.

"Yes," she said.

"You better." He pulled his dick out and she opened her mouth. "Now swallow that shit." She looked him in the eyes and did as he commanded.

• • •

"What happened to your lip?" Monday asked Kenyatta as he walked through the bedroom door, hating that she felt relieved to see him. She noticed that his clothes were disheveled, but she no longer had the energy to stress about where he'd been.

"I ran into the door," he said, looking at the way her hair swept against her collarbones.

Taken aback, she wanted to ask him if the door had beaten his ass, but quickly changed her mind. As she stared at him, his jaw twitched. She swallowed and said, "And how did you do that?"

"I was out thinking and not paying attention when I was walking." He sat on the edge of the bed, the faint scent of Poison perfume lingering on him. Monday diverted her eyes from his face. She couldn't take any more of his lies. She didn't want to argue, and she didn't want to feel stupid that she was lying here on the bed accepting this.

Kenyatta cupped her chin and turned her back toward him. "Monday, baby, I'm just so fucked up about what's going on between us. I need you, baby. You don't understand."

Monday still refused to look in his eyes. "Kenyatta . . . please."

Kenyatta paid Monday no attention as he began to massage her toffee thighs, the soft palms of his hands melting her resistance. He turned her over and she looked at him. Monday hated that looking at him always turned her on, but this time she fought like hell against the feeling that his kissing her inner thigh was giving her. And instead she remembered her conversation with Collyn.

Kenyatta looked at Monday and he could see the brush of coldness on her face. "So what, you don't want me to touch you?"

"No," she spoke quietly, holding her voice steady, "I don't." She clicked off the lamp on the nightstand and the room suddenly went dark.

FOURTEEN

"Have you heard from Kenyatta, baby?" Bless said, as he held Collyn's floor-length blue chinchilla open for her to slide her arms into, "I've been calling him and he hasn't returned any of my calls."

Collyn's curls bounced as she turned her head toward him. "Why would I ever want to hear from Kenyatta?" She pulled her coat closed and tucked her Chloe clutch under her arm.

Bless laughed. "I was just wondering." He was dressed in a black tuxedo. "First, he's on the news about the chick missing, and now, he's misappropriating city money. That's some crazy shit."

Collyn said, taken aback, "I don't remember that."

"What, the missing chick?"

"Not that, the misappropriating money, when did you hear that?"

Bless paused, "Read it, a few days ago in the paper."

"Hmph," Collyn said as if she were in deep thought. "But I'm not surprised."

"Nah? But what about the missing girl scandal. What do you think of that?"

Collyn bit the corner of her lip. She started to tell Bless that Eve was one of her top girls and she was convinced that Kenyatta had something to do with her disappearance, but since she never allowed anyone besides her cousin Taryn into her business, instead she said, "I don't wanna talk about Kenyatta. It is what it is."

"True." He looked her up and down. "Damn, you look good."

"Don't get any ideas." She laughed as they walked out the door, headed for the opera. " 'Cause you won't be getting any pussy."

"Shit, you a lie," he said as they waited for the valet to bring his Navigator around. "Got my ass up in this tux and shit."

Collyn playfully mushed him in the head, "Shut up."

"What I do?"

"Nothing." She kissed him. "Nothing."

As they rode along the highway Collyn wondered how were Kenyatta and Monday making out. She hadn't heard anything from the feds so she hoped it was a sign that they would be leaving her alone, but she wasn't sure.

"Bless," Collyn played with the lapel of his tuxedo jacket. "When's the last time you've seen Kenyatta?"

"I told you, in a minute. Why?"

"Well, when you were with him, did he ever mention anyone named Tracy?"

"Tracy?" he arched his eyebrows, "Nah, never. Who is that?"

"I don't know."

"You don't know? And you expect me to?"

"It's crazy, I know, but I just thought maybe you'd heard him call that name or something."

Bless looked at Collyn and he could tell that there was more to the story than what she just told him, but for argument's sake, he was willing to let it go. "All right Collyn, if you say so." He said as they pulled in front of NJPAC.

They arrived at the opera, where an entire who's who was in attendance. After some mingling Collyn snickered to herself at some of the celebrities and politicians, who seemed nervous around her because they had utilized her business.

Collyn and Bless enjoyed the cocktail hour and the pre-show performance by a world renowned orchestra. Afterward they went to their enclosed box seats, with reclining burgundy leather chairs, wine chilling in a platinum ice bucket, and surround sound in the ceiling that made it seem as if they were on stage.

A minute later the house lights went down and the show began.

"Yo'," Bless leaned over and whispered, "you have any panties on?"

"See, you play too much," Collyn said as Bless eased the sides of her dress up, running his hands up her thighs and along the curves of her ass.

Kissing her on the neck, Bless said, "You wet?"

Collyn smacked his hand. "What did I tell you?"

"Look, if I ain't gettin' no pussy, I can go home, 'cause I don't even know what they sayin'." He nodded toward the stage.

"Blessing, would you behave?"

"I am, but I'm sayin', though, let's play a game." He felt between her inner thighs.

"What game?"

"Let me see if I can make you hit some of those operatic high notes. And you know you got this chick beat. Remember the other night, you were like 'Ahhhhh—' "

She clapped her hands over his mouth. "Are you crazy? What has gotten into you?"

"Man, just give me some pussy and stop playing with me. I'm gettin' tired now."

Collyn hesitated for a moment. "If I give you a little bit, would you let me watch the show?"

"Hell yeah, 'cause I'ma go to sleep afterward."

"I can't take you anywhere," she said, standing up, giving him a moment to unzip his pants and free his hard-on.

Collyn reached over, pulled the velvet curtain to give them a little more privacy, and then returned to his lap.

"I knew you had a thong on." He pushed her pearl thong to the side and eased his thick, long pipe into her warm center. "Ahh, that's better, now this is how you enjoy the opera." He placed his hands on her hips and assisted her with gyrating them. The smooth skin on her ass felt like butter against his thighs as Bless found himself doing his damnedest not to bend her completely over and hit it from the back. Her center was always so inviting, so luscious, and so warm that he found himself placing his fingers on her clit and caressing it, while she swirled discreetly on his dick.

Collyn bit the corner of her lip as Bless's rock solid member felt as if it were melting every ounce of sugar from her walls. She could feel her candy sliding down the thumping veins on the side. She grabbed the arms of the chair, sucked in a breath, and released a scream that would put the most prestigious opera singer to rest.

"Collyn," Bless whispered, "you gon' get us locked up and shit." He laughed, "Calm down."

Collyn looked around to see if they had gathered any on-lookers, seeing none she continued on, bucking his jimmy until she felt Bless's thighs become tense, causing him to bite her lightly on the shoulder and whisper her name while he came, releasing his white chocolate into her flesh.

After they went into the private bathroom and freshened up, there was enough time left in the show for Collyn to enjoy it and, as promised, for Bless to get his nap on.

Three hours later, the opera ended and they headed home.

"Did you have a good time?" she asked as he held the door open for her.

"Hated it," he said, now sitting behind the wheel.

"What?"

"Hell yeah, you were real stingy."

"Stingy? We were sitting in five-hundred-dollar seats and all you did was badger me for pussy and then you took your ungrateful ass to sleep." She laughed, "You are so selfish."

"Selfish? You only gave me a little bit."

Collyn scooted over. "Aw, my sweetie feels neglected?" She unzipped his pants.

"Maybe."

"Don't be like that." She eased his thick head into her mouth. "Mama didn't mean it."

Bless blew air out the side of his mouth, "Damn girl, you don't be playing." He did his best to keep his eyes on the road as she licked the length and nearly caused him to miss the brake pedal.

Bless was struggling like hell to keep his eyes steady on the road. "Goddamn, baby."

She lifted her eyes. "I'm just trying not to be stingy."

Before he could respond she took him back into her mouth.

"Fuck, hol' up." He pulled over to a wooded area off the shoulder. The night air was pitch black, with yellow and red lights streaking by from the passing cars along the highway.

"What are you doing?" Collyn gave his dick one last kiss.

"Take that shit off," Bless said, removing his tuxedo jacket. "That's enough of you fuckin' wit' me. Get yo' ass in the back."

"Bless—"

"Bless hell. Get yo' ass in the back and take that shit off. All of it."

"Why don't we wait until we get home?"

"Home? I'ma fuck you when we get home too. Don't worry about that, I got home covered."

Collyn climbed in the back and flattened the seats. She pulled her dress over her head and threw it to the front. Bless stripped out of his tux and kicked off his shoes. "Where them panties at? And take off that bra too."

"Bless, what if we get caught?"

"Don't worry, I got bail money."

Collyn giggled, loving how he made her feel sixteen again.

Finally climbing into the back, Bless drew her lips into a deep, soulful kiss while his hard cock rubbed against her throbbing clit. Their tongues danced together in an erotic rhythm that elevated Collyn's body temperature. Spreading her legs wide, Bless slipped in one finger and twirled it inside her wetness, causing her to moan.

"Goddamn, look at how wet you are," he said, sliding in a second finger. "How you gon' tell me you weren't gon' give me none of this pussy?" He slid a third finger inside her and started pumping. Collyn lifted her hips and matched the rhythm of his fingers.

"Pussy over here callin' my name," Bless continued.

"Baby, I was just playin'."

"Playin', huh? Well, let me show you how I play." He eased

down her belly, French-kissed her navel, and continued on to placing sloppy wet kisses in, out, and in between her center. "Hold them fat lips open." He kissed them. "Hold 'em open," he commanded.

Collyn reached down and spread her pussy lips, giving him room to lick all of it all while his fingers continued to pump in and out of her.

"That'll teach you to play with me." His tongue quickened its pace, causing her first orgasm to kiss his lips.

"Roll over," he instructed her.

She obeyed and lay on her belly.

He rubbed his hardness across her ass and slowly eased his dick in. Collyn threw her head back, and a sigh of relief fell from her lips.

He reached forward, gave her breasts a hard squeeze, and thrust into her. Her ass bounced against his shaft, and in no time at all the Navigator was rocking on the side of the highway and she was screaming his name.

"That's right, baby, show me how much you want it." He pounded, her ass popping against him. "Shit, I'm 'bout cum." His thrusting quickened. Collyn screamed and her sugar walls collapsed.

A second later, Bless growled out his release and collapsed against her back, whispering, "This shit is dangerous."

FIFTEEN

Monday stood in the parlor watching Kenyatta in the kitchen as he leaned against the picture window. It had been close to five months since Eve disappeared and Kenyatta was still telling the same lie. Nothing had changed, only the day.

Monday walked softly into the kitchen before realizing Kenyatta was on the phone. "I can't see you tonight," he said, causing her to stop dead in her tracks. "Look, I know you want to be with me. But not right now, tomorrow."

"Why can't you be with the bitch now?" Monday spat. She knocked him on his shoulder, causing him to fall forward against the picture window.

He quickly turned around. "What the fuck—?"

"Oh, you cussin' at me and you got some bitch on the

phone? You tryna flex for a bitch?" Monday ran toward him and snatched the phone. "Who the fuck is this?" she screamed into the receiver, and the person quickly hung up. Monday turned to Kenyatta and flung the phone at him, barely missing the maid, who had come into the kitchen. Immediately Monday apologized. "Mary, I'm so sorry."

"But wat de hell is dis?" Mary spat in a thick Trinidadian accent. She looked at the phone that had slammed against the floor so hard it was in pieces. Her golden face was red as she blinked. "Jesus." She made the sign of the cross on her chest. "You know if dat woulda hit me in me head we woulda had a problem." She sucked her teeth long and hard.

Monday and Kenyatta both stopped dead in their tracks and blinked. Mary had been with them for years, and though they knew she was from Trinidad, they'd never thought about it, at least until now. After clearing her throat, Mary quickly returned to her role. "Ms. Hudson James is here to see you."

Kenyatta frowned and his eyes revealed that he was taken aback. "What?"

Although Mary was doing her best to be polite, it was obvious that she wasn't in the mood for his shit. "Would you like me to show her in?"

"Oh, it's okay," Hudson said as she stormed into the kitchen with a milky white stain running down the front of her blouse. She walked over to the sink and wet a paper towel. Cleaning herself, she said, "Thanks, Mary."

"Are you still breast-feeding?" Monday snapped.

"No." Hudson frowned. "It's from the baby's bottle."

"I take it I can leave now." Mary nodded and excused herself.

"We should just get to the point," Hudson said. "I spoke with Mehki and a few of the other attorneys and it doesn't look good. We should've thought this out before we decided to fire

Charles. Because now the feds want to do an audit and I'm not sure how things are looking."

"I told you, you shouldn't have done that anyway," Monday said.

"Monday," Kenyatta said, "this doesn't concern you."

Monday looked at Hudson, embarrassed about the way her husband had spoken to her, "Who are you talking to?"

"Don't question me, Monday."

"Excuse me—" Mary interrupted.

"What?" they all snapped, and Mary stepped back.

She swallowed. "There's a Mr. Bless Shields here to see you, sir."

"What is he doing here?" Kenyatta arched his eyebrows.

"I invited him," Hudson said. "Thanks, Mary. Show him in."

"Why the hell is she inviting people to our house?" Monday exclaimed.

Kenyatta turned to Monday. "Chill."

"Whatever." She stormed over to the counter and poured herself a glass of water.

Bless walked into the kitchen, and Monday frowned at him.

Bless smirked. "I'm fine and you?"

Monday shot him a quick fake smile. "I'm well."

"I can tell." Bless nodded toward Hudson and gave Kenyatta a handshake. "I've been trying to reach you for a minute. Where have you been?"

"A little tied up. Wassup?"

"What do you mean, wassup? I got a call from my assistant last night who said that you needed the signed contracts today."

"Me?" Kenyatta said, surprised.

"Yes," Hudson answered. "I thought we needed them so that the waterfront construction can already be in operation when the books are looked at."

"You gave him another contract?" Monday snapped.

"What the fuck did I just tell you?" Kenyatta squinted at Monday, "You gon' mess around and I'ma make you go upstairs."

"Make me? Well maybe you should, because I really need to see this."

"Excuse us." Kenyatta looked at Monday and grabbed her by the arm. He walked her roughly into the hall. "What the fuck is your problem?"

"When the hell did you get disrespectful to the point where you think you can talk to me like that? I don't appreciate that shit! I'm not that missing-ass ho in the street. I'm your wife!"

Kenyatta cleared his throat. "Then act like my wife and shut the fuck up."

"What?" Monday felt like he'd just backhanded her. "I can't believe I was still looking out for your benefit and here you are . . . you will never change."

"Looking out for my benefit how?" he said sarcastically, "by nagging me?"

"Fuck you." And she turned away.

Kenyatta snatched her back, "What are you talking about? What do you mean looking out for my benefit?"

Monday hesitated. She wanted to spit in his face, but there was something in his eyes and everytime she looked at him, she felt like this would be the one time she could save him . . . even if it was from himself. "I shouldn't tell your ass shit. I should let Hudson do her job—"

"Would you just say it!"

"Look, it's not personal, because I don't know him like that, but if you want to work with him and he's really cool, then have him set up a front, a business that doesn't seem as if he owns it."

"Why?" Kenyatta asked, genuinely interested.

"This way no one can say you're setting up bids and getting kickbacks. The company will look new and it'll seem like you're giving everyone a chance."

Kenyatta paced for a moment and tapped his foot. Why hadn't he thought of the front? He looked at her, turned around and left her standing there. He went back to the kitchen, and she heard him tell Hudson and Bless everything she'd just said, as if it were his idea. Hudson said, "I'll get right on that." Even in her home, she was on the outside looking in. But then again, this was the mayor's mansion.

She could hear their laughter and Kenyatta's spin on her ideas bounce around the room as she went upstairs grabbed her purse, and left.

SIXTEEN

The cool evening air blew into Monday's mahogany face, and her hair whipped along the sides of her cheeks as she rode through Harlem, thinking, sightseeing, and appreciating its beauty.

Monday pulled into the parking lot of Eunice's, a small diner that she and Kenyatta frequented when they first moved to New York. Gladys Knight and the Pips' "Midnight Train to Georgia" played over the sound system as the waitress asked her, "How are you today, Mrs. Smith?"

"I'm fine, thank you."

"Well, it's nice to see you here."

Monday smiled. She hadn't heard that in a while. "Thank you."

"Would you like anything to drink?"

"A cold Uptown please."

"You got it." The waitress left the table and Monday heard her say, "Hey, Mehki, your order is at the counter."

Monday quickly turned around. His back was facing her.

"Working late?" The waitress asked him as she stepped behind the register and rang up his total.

"Yeah." He smiled, "You know how it is, a black man's work is never done."

The waitress blushed, "Especially one who works as hard as you."

Monday smirked. She wasn't sure if she was pissed that the waitress was flirting with him or that he seemed to be enjoying it. She did what she could to suppress the jealousy that crept into her chest, besides—no matter how fine he was and how much her pussy ached and her nipples hardened at the sight of him—she was married—but then again, what the fuck did that mean?

She watched Mehki grab the white plastic bag, which contained his food and had THANK YOU written in red letters across it. He winked his eye at the waitress and turned toward the door.

As he left and the door swung behind him, his silk tie hung loosely around his neck and the cuffs of his starched sage shirt were flipped up to his elbows. The beautifully dark waves in his hair spun like a charismatic rhythm, while the sexiness of his body always spoke for itself.

He crossed the street and walked into a tall and all brick office building with floor to ceiling windows, black metal railings, a copper awning above the door, and an all glass entrance, which read in gold script: DAVIS, PARKER, AND LASSITER, ATTORNEYS AT LAW.

Damn, Monday thought as she immediately became torn between being Kenyatta's faithful yet neglected wife or fulfilling an aching and ambiguous yearning for something different than her marriage and the man she chose. It's not that she didn't love her husband or want to make her marriage work, but given all the things that had been happening, she wondered what was she really working for. And the more Kenyatta did things that made her question why she loved him, and the more he lied and continued to lie, the more disrespectful he became, and the more he disregarded her, the more she wanted to test the waters and see . . . if just maybe . . . this pretty motherfucker, Mehki, was exactly who his swagger represented him to be.

"Anything else?" the waitress said, cutting through her thoughts and placing her drink on the table.

"No, thank you." Monday said, never taking her eyes from the building, "This is fine." She wrapped her fingers around the cold glass and the melting frost moistened her palms and slid over her fingers. Monday held the rim of the glass to her chin, wondering if she had anything more to lose than her curiosity. Deciding that at least at this moment she didn't, she placed ten dollars on the table and left.

A few moments later she was standing in front of a dark mahogany door with a gleaming silver and engraved nameplate that read, MEHKI DAVIS, ESQ.

Monday sucked in her stomach and tugged a little at the hem of her teal strapless dress that gathered slightly around the breasts and had a midthigh pencil skirt that rode her hips just right. Her four-inch Manolos made her apple bottom look beyond ripe. She held her matching trench coat in the crux of her right arm and her petite Chanel purse in the palm of her left hand.

She knocked lightly on the door at first and then a little harder.

"Good night, Helen." Mehki yelled from behind the door, "I'll see you in the morning."

Monday knocked again.

"I know," he said, "I won't be here all night, and yes," he laughed, "I have something good to eat."

"Is it as good as me?" Monday twisted the knob and opened the door.

"Damn," a sexy and surprised smile lit up Mehki's face as the setting sun glowed behind him. "That all depends," he took his rimless glasses off and placed them on his desk. "If I ever have the pleasure of being reminded again." He took a drag from the cigar which hung from the corner of his mouth and released the smoke from his lips in slow motion.

"Mmmm, perhaps." Monday rested her coat and purse in the chair by the door while she threw a dash more of motion in her ocean. She walked over to his large cherrywood desk and sat on the corner. She crossed her thick thighs, turned to face him, and slid the cigar he smoked from the corner of his mouth and into hers. She took a pull. "I've been thinking a lot about you."

Mehki rose from his seat, locked his office door, and then he rolled his burgundy leather wing chair directly in front of her, laid back, and watched as she took a toke from the cigar and the smoke snaked from between her glistening MAC covered lips.

"Really?" His eyes combed her smooth and beautifully brown legs. He ran his hands over her shins and up her thighs, "Is that so?"

She held the cigar between her fingers like a cigarette, "Of course that's so."

"And why is that?" He took the cigar from between her fingers, took a pull, and mashed it into the marble ashtray.

"Because." Monday lifted the tie from around his neck, "I have." She began unbuttoning his shirt and running her hands over his defined chest, caressing his nipples, straddling his lap, and gyrating her hips across the monstrous mountain in his pants.

He looked her dead in the eyes, "You know I've missed you over the years."

A surge of chills ran up Monday's legs and hung out in her chest; she backed up and he pulled her toward him. "But I need you to tell me what are you doing here?"

"I wanted to be here." She drew her face into his and he kissed her as if he'd been desiring this kiss forever, yet in the midst of it, he stopped, "Wait a minute."

"Why did you stop?" she asked, taken aback.

"Because, I need to know what you're doing here?"

"Why do you keep asking me that?"

"Because I want to know. Don't you think you owe me an explanation, especially after all these years?"

"If you want me to leave," she backed up and again he pulled her toward him, "I can go. I just thought that maybe," she playfully bit his chin, "I would show you that I wanted some of this." She moved her hips.

"Monday, you wanting to fuck me is nothing new." He cupped her breasts and massaged his thumbs into her hard nipples, "As a matter of fact, every time you see me, you wanna make love to me. And I wanna make love to you. But not until today have you ever come on this strong, and now you expect me to believe that it's only because you've been thinking about me? Come on, Monday, it's me."

"So . . . what . . . you don't want any?"

"Oh, I want all of it, you can believe that," he caressed her thighs and kissed her lips. "But first I need to understand why you're giving it to me."

"It's an affair."

"An affair is a series of fucks that happen more than once, is that what you want? Or you wanna get turned out for a night and then sent home?"

Monday hesitated. She didn't know, she hadn't thought beyond right now. All she knew is that at this moment she needed him. She caressed the sides of his face and knew that despite what they'd been through he could be trusted with her innermost secrets. She knew he was well aware of Kenyatta and probably knew more about him than she did, but still she wasn't sure if she wanted only a little bit or more. "I don't have an answer to that. What do you want?"

"To give you whatever it is you need."

Monday was taken aback. "Why would you want to do that? Even after what I did to you."

"Monday, don't you know that I know you, that I knew you and I knew you felt like you had to get away? The only thing is, I knew you were running from yourself, but you didn't."

"I tried, but it didn't work."

"Because it's like trying to outrun the sky, you can't do it."

"But I just . . ." she paused, "I just want to so bad."

"Why do you still want to do that?"

"Because of the situation I'm in. I'm just tired of being lied to."

"I know you are, that's why I want you to be honest with me. And tell me what you need."

"I just need to be held right now."

He placed his arms around her waist and she moved in closer to his chest. "And right now . . ." she whispered while caressing one side of his face, sucking his earlobe, and placing soft kisses along the side of his neck, "I just want you to make love to me."

Mehki reached behind her and unzipped her dress, the top portion falling over her perfectly round and erect breasts.

"Damn, they're beautiful." He took her breasts squeezed and slid them between his lips, where he alternated kisses, sucks, tugs, pulls, and pops.

Monday closed her eyes. She enjoyed listening to the rhythm of his mouth moving forcefully, yet graciously across her nickel-sized nipples. Monday was sure when Mehki was done her breasts would be swollen. He laid her back on the desk and slid her dress completely off. Standing over her he asked, "Are you sure you want to do this?"

She sat up and unbuckled his pants, "Yes."

Monday kissed him all over his body as he undressed. Once his clothes were removed she straddled him. "Damn, this a big dick." She rotated her hips.

"That's why you wanted it."

"I promise I won't leave you again."

"You will, which is why this time, we're going to be friends with benefits."

"Mehki . . ."

"Why you start talking so much when we're trying to fuck." He stood up and laid her back on the desk. He stroked her twice, pulled out, and entered her again. He continued to repeat the process, leaving her mind spent. Every time he opened her up she felt a surge of wind invade her body and send pricks through her skin. Yet, she loved every bit of it, especially the teasing game that he was playing.

Mehki stood back and watched her lava run between her thighs. He rubbed his dick in it and then entered her again, this time not stopping.

After a few minutes of their rekindled rhythm, each of them recalling how the other liked for them to move, Mehki crossed Monday's legs Indian style across his chest, as his dick ran a marathon between her lower lips.

Monday screamed as he whipped his hips like a tornado's

wind. He held her legs back over her head, opening her up completely, knocking her walls back and erotically carving her pussy into the shape that he wanted it in. "If you fuck Kenyatta after this," he stroked, "he gon' know I been here." He flipped her to the side.

"Mehki." Monday's head tossed and turned, "Damn this feels so good. Shit." She turned over, he lifted her from his desk and bounced her on his dick.

BAM! A forceful knock beat against the door while the locked knob twisted, "Mehki, I saw your car outside, it's Kenyatta. I need to speak to you, it's important." He twisted the locked knob again, "Open up."

Monday's heart sank in her chest as Mehki placed Monday on the desk, but instead of stopping like she thought he would, he flipped her over and continued fucking her. She turned her head to the side, "What if he hears us?"

"If you stop screaming he won't."

"Maybe you should get that. Maybe I should hide."

"He gon' wait until I'm done fucking you." Mekhi resumed his strokes, "Kenyatta, I'm on a call, can it wait until the morning?"

"No, I need to speak to you right now."

"You'll . . ." Mehki stroked while his eyes were half-staff, ". . . have . . . to wait."

"Ai'ight man. I'll be right here."

Mehki flipped Monday back over to face him and pulled her onto his lap while he sat in the chair, "I don't want you to ever feel unworthy again."

She looked him in the eyes, "I won't."

"Anything you need I got it."

"Don't make me promises. Just show me." She began to pant as his chest started to heave. Both of their pelvises contracted, and while he shot his love into her like Cupid's arrow, she rained hers onto him.

"Damn," she sighed, breathing heavy, "I don't want this to end. I swear I want some more."

With Monday still on his lap, Mehki grabbed his pants and handed her his apartment keys. "1153 Lenox, apartment 13C, meet me there."

She looked at him seriously, "And how am I going to get out of here?"

Mehki smiled, "That's what back doors are for."

DOWN LOW WITH
FLATS ON

SEVENTEEN

She sat on the fire escape, the late October breeze ruffling the white nylon of her see-through negligee. The rusted metal felt cold on the back of her thighs, and the persistent wind blew loose strands of her hair directly into the low O's of smoke she eased from the center of her dry mouth.

She could hear the baby crying as her eyes burned. Yet she fought with all she had to keep them open, wondering why Kenyatta had lied yet again. The more he lied, the more unraveled she became.

And it wasn't so much his fucking her that kept her going as it was his scent . . . his voice . . . his hands . . . his swagger . . . his full lips that curled when he laughed. It was him. Just being in his presence turned her on. It didn't matter that he said they needed space—whatever the fuck that was—or that things between them were pretty much over. What mattered is he kept coming around, calling her, fucking her, laughing with her, pacifying her, and agreeing that things would get better. He continued to be her shoulder to lean on. So as far as she was concerned, nothing had changed.

So where was he? And why wasn't he answering his phone or returning any of her voice messages . . . or apologizing for making her feel like a whole new level of shit? She'd had his baby, and she'd gotten rid of Eve; nevertheless, none of that was enough.

She sniffed and sucked the butt of her cigarette like a stick of weed. "He thinks that I'm a fuckin' joke." She flicked away the loose snot that ran from her nose. "Like I'm some sorta game. Like my feelings ain't shit." She stood up and spoke into the wind, the fire escape rattling as she paced. "Like he doesn't remember chasing me the fuck around . . . banging down my door . . . promising me what the fuck he would do for me. 'I love you, it's gon' be me and you. Just trust me . . . let your guard down. I know you may have been hurt in the past, but this is me.' " She poked herself in the chest, the ashes from her burning cigarette falling at her feet.

"And now all of a sudden"—she waved her hand as if she were pulling a rabbit from a hat—"he doesn't want me?" She wiped the blinding tears from her eyes. "Now all of a sudden he flexin'?" She paced, her bare feet feeling numb against the cold metal. She desperately tried to calm herself, but she couldn't get past feeling like *this,* the indescribable *this* that clogged her throat and sliced every artery that lined the center of her chest, where she desired to have more, to be treated better, and to be left alone to handle *this* fucked-up feeling on her own hung out. *This* feeling that somehow compromised her into accepting the very shit she'd sworn to her girlfriends that she would never contend with.

Yet here she stood, practically naked, on the fire escape with wild hair framing her face like a lion's mane, swearing that today would be the day that hell would rain down.

EIGHTEEN

Live jazz radiated through Collyn's gallery. She was hosting a black-tie reception showcasing an array of exquisite and exclusive artistic pieces. White-gloved butlers in tuxedos served champagne, caviar, and sushi while several artists walked the floor, giving tours to small gatherings of people.

Collyn's off-white floor-length gown flowed and the baguettes in her ears gleamed as she glanced at the clock, wondering where Bless was. He'd been due at the gallery over an hour ago and had yet to show up or to call her. She wondered if he was even going to make it.

"Collyn," Taryn said, running in breathlessly and kissing her on the cheek, "sorry, I ran late. The sitter had a little car trouble getting to my house, so I had to take the baby to her."

"It's fine. Pierre was a big help." Collyn smiled. "You look beautiful, though."

"Well, thank you." Taryn, who was a dead ringer for Jill Scott, playfully batted her eyelashes. "You know I have to hold it down for the big girls."

Collyn laughed, then she and Taryn mingled with the guests and answered their questions. After about an hour of mingling, Collyn whispered to Taryn as they stood in a far corner and sipped champagne, "Let me ask you something."

"Sure."

"Have you been talking to Kenyatta?"

"No," Taryn said without hesitation.

Collyn stared at Taryn, "Why would you lie to me?"

Taryn sighed, "Look . . . we started messing around again. And . . . I couldn't do it anymore. It was too much—the lying—the women—his wife."

"So how come you never told me this?"

"I know how you are and I just didn't feel like hearing it, plus I know how crazy I looked messing around with him again."

Collyn hesitated, "Did you . . . did you stop messing with him before or after Eve disappeared?"

"Before, way before."

"I hope so Taryn . . ." Collyn's voice trailed off, "I really hope so."

"Why'd you say that?" Taryn snapped, "What is that supposed to mean? You don't think," she pointed to her chest, "that I did something—?"

"Did you?"

"Hell no, did you?"

"I didn't have a reason to."

"Me either—and besides, I would've had his ass disappear." Taryn laughed.

Collyn snickered, "You wrong for that."

"Seriously, though," Taryn said, "you think something happened to her?"

"Yeah," Collyn said as she watched the FBI agents, who'd come to her gallery before, walk in. "I do now."

"What do they want?" Taryn asked, concerned.

"I guess we'll soon find out." Collyn smiled as the agents walked up to her.

She held her hand out, and Agent Jones accepted her gesture. "Ms. Bazemore," he said, looking her over and smiling, his eyes clearly revealing that he liked what he saw. "Seems we meet again." He grinned.

"Seems so." She smiled back. "Would you like to step into my office, gentlemen?"

"Actually, there's no need. You just need to come with us."

"Excuse me?" Collyn said while continuing to smile, the slight tremble in her voice letting them know she'd been caught off guard.

"We can do this nicely," Agent West said, nodding at a passing guest, "or we can do it another way."

Collyn swallowed as she turned to Taryn, who said, "What do they mean, you have to go with them?"

Collyn arched her eyebrows and shook her head. The look in her eyes told Taryn to calm down. "Call my attorney for me and have her meet me at the federal building, and then—"

"Collyn—"

Collyn gave Taryn the look again. "And then," she went on, "continue to host the party and I will call you when the gentlemen and I are done." She could tell that Taryn was uneasy. "Okay?"

"Yes."

Collyn turned to the agents, "After you."

"Ladies first." The three of them walked out the door, slid into the gray Crown Victoria, and disappeared into the night.

• • •

Once they arrived at the federal building, Collyn was escorted to an interrogation room, where her attorney awaited her arrival.

The agents pulled out a chair for Collyn. She sat down while they sat on the edge of the metal table across from her. Her attorney sat at her side.

"Can you please explain to us what this is about?" Evelyn Cochran, Collyn's attorney, asked the agents.

"We need information." Agent Jones smiled, "I'm certain you understand that, Counselor. So, how about we begin?" He looked at Collyn. "Do you know Eve Johnson?"

"I know quite a few Johnsons, Agent. We've had this discussion already."

"Hmmm, Ms. Bazemore, how about this: we have Eve's diary that says you know exactly who she is."

"This is not another one of that 'five witnesses' type of thing, is it? Because if you have it in print, then what do you need my explanation for?"

Agent Jones looked at Collyn's attorney. "Perhaps you need to get your client to understand that we're not playing. We will have her sitting in detention so fast her head will spin. Now, do you need a moment to recollect or has your memory suddenly cleared up?"

Collyn's attorney looked at her and nodded, indicating she should cooperate. "Yes, I know Eve Johnson," she responded.

"Great," Agent West said. "Now, did Mayor Kenyatta Smith solicit sex from your business? And before you perjure yourself and we have to charge you with something we're not really interested in, let me tell you what we know for sure. You've always been wealthy, but this is the wealthiest you've ever been. You were born to be a madam and to run your family business, which you've been doing since college, because that was right about the time that your mother retired and moved back to a tiny island that your family owns a few miles off the coast of Jamaica. Ya know whutta mean, mun?" he said in an enhanced Jamaican accent. "You're an only child, and the only other family you have here in the States is your cousin Taryn and her child, your godchild. You run an upscale art gallery that covers for the exquisite pussy that you have for sale. Now you may answer the question."

"What do you want from me?" Collyn suppressed the panic in her voice.

"The truth. Now, on to Mayor Kenyatta Smith."

"What about him?"

"Do you know him?"

"Yes."

"Was he a client of yours?"

"No."

They raised their eyebrows. "You are aware that we already know the answers?"

"My client just answered your question, agents," Collyn's attorney said.

"No, your client just lied," Agent Jones snapped. "Let's try this again: did Mayor Kenyatta Smith ever solicit services from Eve Johnson while she worked at Red Light Special?"

Collyn sat silently. She knew that all of this was bullshit, otherwise they would be charging her with solicitation or whatever shit they could come up with. Besides, if they had the truth in print, then why would they be asking her any questions? "No," Collyn said, calling their bluff, "I don't recall ever doing business with Mayor Smith."

"And that's your final answer?"

"Yes, it is."

"Okay."

"So, now that my client has answered your questions, we're going to ask you if you're through," Evelyn said.

"For now," Agent West said. "But I can promise you that we'll be seeing you two again."

Collyn and her attorney rose from their chairs. "Evening, gentlemen."

"Evenin', Ms. Bazemore."

NINETEEN

Collyn crept quietly into her apartment, still shaken from her interrogation by the FBI. She wondered where Bless was and why he hadn't shown up. She'd called him at least a million times and hadn't heard from him yet. This was an example of why she'd never wanted to get caught up. She removed her gown, hung it up in the closet, went into the bathroom, and began drawing her bath. As she threw a few rose petals into the water her phone rang. It was security, informing her that Bless was downstairs. Collyn sighed. She hated that her heart wanted to see him more than her mind did, because even as her mind said to send his ass home, her heart demanded that she have him come up.

Reluctantly she said to Adam, "Send him up." Turning the water off, she slid into her blue silk robe and walked to the door. As she opened the door, Bless was standing there smiling. He tilted his head to the side and moved his face in for a kiss. Collyn backed away. "Are you serious? Where the hell you been?"

"I ran late, beautiful."

"Whatever." She walked away. "See, this is exactly why I don't like to sweat no niggah, because it's always some bullshit. All of a sudden you're running late, but when you want some pussy I don't have a problem looking up and yo' ass is right there."

"Where I'm 'spose to be if I want some pussy?"

"Is that your attempt at being funny?"

"I'm sorry, baby."

"Fuck your sorry. Shit. This whole day has been a mess. The FBI shows up—"

"Slow down. What do you mean, the FBI showed up? Showed up and what?"

"More of Kenyatta's bullshit."

"What happened?"

"They said they found Eve's diary and asked if Kenyatta was a client of mine. I don't have time for that bullshit!"

"I don't get it. So what's the connection with you, Eve, and Kenyatta? Was she one of your girls?"

Collyn hesitated, "Yeah."

Bless paused. "So what did you tell the FBI?"

"What do you mean?" she said, taken aback. "I ain't tell 'em a motherfuckin' thing. They full of shit anyway. The last time they lied and said they had five people who said I knew Eve, so please, I'm not falling for no diary nonsense. They're too busy trying to get me caught up . . . And anyway, back to your ass." Collyn walked toward the door, cracked it open, and said, "Thank you for stopping by, but good night."

Bless looked at Collyn and laughed. He walked toward the door and closed it. "I ain't going nowhere, ma." Bless pulled Collyn toward him by the ends of her robe's belt. "I'm sorry, my baby. You're right. I should've called and been more considerate. My fault." He began kissing her from her earlobe down her neck. "I promise that if there's a next time, I'll call."

Collyn turned her head away and resisted Bless' attempts to kiss her. "Oh, you don't wanna kiss me?" He untied the belt on her robe and kissed her from the base of her neck down to her breasts. "I know what I can kiss and it won't turn me away." Collyn winced as he bit her nipple. "Hurt?"

"A little."

"You forgive me?"

Silence.

"Aw, my baby." He continued to suck and lick, apologizing with every stroke of his tongue.

He worked his way down, French-kissing between her thighs. "You know I'ma kiss you until you forgive me?" He licked all over her shaved middle.

Afterward he took her hand and slid her fingers along with his into her heated vulva, smearing her wetness on her clit and then licking it off her fingertip. "You forgive me." He dipped her fingers back into her slit and sucked her dripping candy off the tips again. "Damn, this shit is so fuckin' sweet." He opened her up and her wetness glistened like diamonds.

Collyn looked down at him as he took her hand and held one side of her pussy open while taking the other hand and playing with her clit. Bless was so close that his nose was practically buried in it. Collyn pumped in and out of her slit while he sucked her coated fingers and licked her pussy's pinkness. Just when her body started to electrify, she took her right thigh and threw it over his shoulder. He took her fingers and said, "I want you to play with your pussy in my face until I can catch the cum with my tongue."

Doing as he'd asked Collyn stroked her clit in a circular motion, over and over again, until the orgasmic high climbing her hooded mountain reached its peak and her cum began to seep from between the lips.

"It's dripping, baby."

Bless didn't say a word, instead he opened her up, curled his tongue at the base of her pussy, and her erotic liquid drowned his tongue and flowed like a waterfall into his mouth.

"You forgive me?" he laid her on the floor.

"Maybe." She watched him undress. "You're forgiven."

"I better be, how you gon' be mad at me?" Bless lay on top of Collyn, and as she opened her legs and welcomed him home, she kept her eyes open and attempted to look into his, while his eyes quickly became Asian slits. Collyn studied the deep cappuccino color of his face and wondered when did she fall in love with him. Had it been on one of the nights they sat up until the dawn, watching old Bruce Lee flicks . . . But then again, maybe that wasn't it . . . maybe it was when she told him about her desire to one day have children but not being sure if she wanted to pass her family business on to them. But then again, what about that . . . said love?

Maybe . . . maybe . . . it was the foot massages he gave her, the back rubs, the Chinese food he brought every Wednesday and Friday night. Or maybe it was the no-frills peanut butter choke sandwiches they confessed to each other they both liked. It could've been because she was a Delta and he was a Q, and they both remembered their fresh-steppin' moves. And what about the time he was sick and she ran her business from home to take care of him . . . and the next week she caught whatever he had and he in turn did the same. Somewhere in there . . . in the midst of all of that, love crept up and, in true love fashion, caught her off guard and was now showing its ass. And at this moment Collyn could no longer see what her life would be without this man.

Collyn pushed Bless slightly on the shoulder, turned over and she began to ride him. Her breasts bounced in the air and in and out of Bless' mouth.

As Collyn turned around and began to ride him backwards, cowgirl style, he watched her luscious ass rotate like a whirlwind across his dick.

He could feel her pussy contracting. "Oh damn . . . baby . . . shit." Bless placed his hands on both sides of Collyn's ass and squeezed it like a sandwich. He lifted her ass just a bit and watched her cream drip from her slit onto his dick. "Look at that shit."

"You're so nasty."

"You make me nasty."

He flipped her over and now he lay on top. He looked into her eyes, pressed their lips together, and said, "I love you."

Collyn's heart fluttered a thousand times, as she felt Bless' strokes speeding up, forcing her hips to lift slightly off the bed.

"I love you too." She said as she placed her arms around his neck and he freed himself into her flesh.

TWENTY

As time passed Kenyatta became even more undone. He couldn't eat, couldn't sleep, had lost weight, and the nightmares that he prayed would go away now crept up on him in the day.

He and Monday spent most of their time communicating through silence and eye dances. Him looking at her when she didn't know and her looking at him and trying not to show it. Sometimes they succeeded and at other times they didn't. Monday spent most of her time around him wondering and desperately trying to remember if they'd ever really been more than this. Or if they only survived the last ten years because of their superficial dreams, which once fulfilled, limited what they really liked about each other.

"Can I ask you something, Kenyatta?" Monday said standing beside the bed, fully dressed for the day.

"Monday," he said, obviously aggravated, while sitting on the edge of the bed with one hand on the phone and the other massaging his left temple. "I really don't have time for the desperate housewife shit. Or any other nonsense. So please don't ask me anything that's gon' make me cuss you the fuck out."

Monday swallowed, "I wasn't looking to get into a cussin' match, I really wanted to have a heart-to-heart with you." She hesitated. This was her last attempt at seeing if she were having a sentimental meltdown or preparing a matrimonial eulogy. "Lately, I've just been wondering if you still love me."

"Love you?" Kenyatta jerked his neck back. "Do I look like I want to discuss that? What the fuck? Yeah um hmm . . . I love you, but what does that mean? Hell,"—he stood up and hunched his shoulders—"you ain't never done shit for me—"

"Kenyatta—" she gasped.

"Kenyatta the crack of my ass, do I love you? You're a selfish ass. I been in the goddamn paper every fuckin' day. The political career that *I* worked hard for, that *you* been ridin' high on, is about fuckin' over! I'm holding onto my office by a goddamn string and you wanna discuss being in love? How you even twist yo' ass to walk in here with some bullshit like that? Here I had to deal with this dead bitch, Eve—"

Dead? Monday shook her head, his words burned her ears.

"And where have you been, Monday?" He got in her face. "Huh, do I love you? How about this? Do you love me? Have you treated me the way I deserve to be . . . ?"

Monday felt pricks of spit flying from his mouth as he yelled at the top of his lungs, yet she tuned him out and thought about the last question he hurled at her. She decided that her answer was 'no.' She hadn't loved him the way she should've, because if she did, she would've loved his ass from afar.

While standing here and feeling the heat from his angry words spit into her face, she realized that nothing would change if nothing changed.

But shit, she didn't expect this son of a bitch to turn out like this. She didn't see all of this when she first met him and his smile captivated her. Or on their first date nor the first time they held hands or made love. Who knew that what she thought was perfection would turn out to be so corrupt.

Yet, there was no way she could run again. So maybe she needed to force this shit and make it fit. And yeah she had a law degree, but no one except Kenyatta knew that she didn't take the bar. She was too busy being his campaign manager.

". . . You need to be a woman about yours," Kenyatta continued, "and treat me the way I need to be! Do I love you? That's a good question, Monday, considering you haven't done a damn thing to earn it. City Council wants to have a meeting with me and they won't tell me what the agenda is, but did you know that? Hell no! Because you're too self-consumed. Well, you know what, Monday? Fuck the feds, fuck Eve, and fuck you!"

Kenyatta may not have had a razor but he'd sliced every part of Monday's being.

Before Monday could attempt to say anything the phone rang. Kenyatta grabbed the cordless receiver, "Kenyatta Smith." His mood seemed to quickly change as he gave a hardy laugh, "Hudson, you always know what to say to make me feel better." He walked into the bathroom and slammed the door behind him. The rattling of the door as it slammed into the frame caused Monday to come out of the daze she was in.

She grabbed her purse and headed down the stairs and out the door.

A few moments later she was at Bazemore Gallery. She hated looking Taryn in the face, but it seemed today she would have to.

"Look, Monday." Taryn twisted her lips as Monday stepped to the counter. "I do not want to battle with you."

"I would have to give a damn for it to be a battle." Monday said dismissively. "Now get Collyn."

Taryn cleared her throat as a customer walked up behind Monday. Taryn buzzed Collyn, who was seeing a client in her office. After speaking with Collyn, Taryn said, "Pierre, please show Mrs. Smith to the waiting area in the back."

Monday followed Pierre to the customer's lounge, and a few minutes later Pierre motioned for her to come into Collyn's office. Collyn nodded at Pierre as he closed the door behind Monday.

Monday squinted her eyes at Collyn and was surprised by how flushed she looked, her hair was pulled back into a pony-tail and she had barely any makeup on. She popped two Advils into her mouth and sipped a glass of water.

"Damn," Monday said, "What's wrong with you?"

"Flu, maybe. I don't fuckin' know." Collyn said. "But my ass is sick as shit."

"Maybe you should go home and lie down."

"I have too much work to do. Anyway, wassup?"

Monday hated to say this. "I think Eve is dead."

Collyn popped two more Advils in her mouth. "What? What did you say?"

"Listen," Monday paced, "Kenyatta and I were arguing, and he said he had to 'deal with that dead bitch.' "

"He had to . . . ," Collyn said slowly, "deal with that . . . dead bitch. What does that mean?" her voice drifted.

"He didn't kill her if that's what you're thinking," Monday said defensively. "He wouldn't have done that. He's not a mur-derer. But I wouldn't put it past him to know who is."

"What? A murderer?"

"Yes."

"You don't think—"

"He's not a killer."

"You're awfully defensive."

"Because I know him."

"Do you really? Maybe it was an accident."

"No." Monday shook her head. "He wouldn't have done that. I think he knows the truth and he's hiding it."

"Why?" Collyn leaned forward on both elbows, "Why would he do that? Who would he be protecting?" Collyn slammed her fist into her desk, "I swear to God I hate the day I met that motherfucker!"

Monday flopped down in the chair and held her face in her hands.

"It's something," Collyn said. "I know it is."

"But what if Eve isn't dead?" Monday asked.

"Then she's playing one hell of a fuckin' game with all of us. And if that's the case they won't have to look for her because I'ma kill her ass."

TWENTY-ONE

"I'll have a Heineken," Kenyatta said to the bartender as he spotted Bless sitting at the bar, watching the game. "Blessing." Kenyatta smiled as he shook his hand.

They were in Short Hills, New Jersey, at the exclusive Grandview Country Club, where Kenyatta was a long-time member.

During the hour-long drive from Gracie Mansion to Short Hills, Kenyatta was grateful to get out of the city and clear his mind. For the first time in his political career, he was thinking about tossing shit to the wind, saying fuck it, and giving it all up. He was growing tired of the constant attention that he used to welcome. Where he once loved the public's spotlight and treasured everyone wanting to know him, he now felt on overload, as if he were only seconds away from a political overdose.

Now he wanted simple shit. No more of this bitch and that bitch all pulling him in a million different directions when all he wanted to give them was dick. No more emotional attachments because they'd fallen for some bullshit-ass line he'd given them. All of that was a wrap, because at the end of the day all he had was some skeeted-ass nuts, an unsolved murder, and a buncha goddamn babies.

"Mayor Smith." Bless smiled.

"Good to see you, Bless. Thanks for coming."

"Anytime. I just hope your game is straight." Bless pointed out the picture window to the greens. He made a motion as if he were swinging a golf club. "'Cause I'm the man." He popped his collar.

Kenyatta laughed. "You got on a pink-ass shirt and some khaki pants and you the man? Ai'ight." The bartender handed him his beer.

"Oh, you tryna be funny?" Bless cocked his head.

Kenyatta laughed. "Whatever. Put all that smack in your game."

"Let's do this, then."

"Let's."

Kenyatta finished his beer and they headed out to the greens, where the caddie walked behind them. Once they reached the first tee, Kenyatta took his position and swung his club. They watched where the ball landed. Kenyatta turned toward the caddie and said, "Give us a few minutes."

"Wassup?" Bless said after taking his swing.

"I called you out here because this most recent contract we did will have to be the last one like that," Kenyatta said as they walked toward the balls.

Bless looked at him, taken aback. "Why?"

"Because shit is real crazy right now. The FBI is looking at me. You read the papers, and as you can see, I'm in those motherfuckers damn near every day."

"Yeah, I know. It's like they can't get enough of you. Goes with the territory, I suppose."

"Yeah, maybe. But most of it's stemming from some bullshit."

"What bullshit?" Bless asked.

Kenyatta paused while he took his second swing. For a brief moment he thought about telling Bless the truth about Eve, about Monday, about everything. Hell, he needed somebody to confess to. But as quickly as the thought came, he changed his mind. "The bullshit-ass case an ex-employee has against me."

"The one you fired?" Bless said, not looking up as he swung.

"Yeah, Charles."

"Why'd you fire him?"

"Look, I'll put it to you like this. He was in my business too much, and had he stayed on, there would be no kickbacks and shit. Understand?"

"Well, damn," Bless laughed as they walked toward the hole. "I guess that niggah had to go."

"Exactly. Which is why at least for a while the next set of contracts will have to be legitimate. I don't want any shit."

"I understand."

For the next two hours they played golf, each of them declaring that he'd beaten the other. Afterward they headed back inside to the bar, where Kenyatta had one too many.

"It's a good thing I'm not driving," Kenyatta said, taking his third shot of Patrón to the head and chasing it with a Heineken.

"How'd you get here?"

"I have a driver waiting."

"Oh, ai'ight. Must be nice."

"Yeah, I guess. Before all this bullshit with Eve, I had a driver by choice. Now I need that motherfucker."

"Eve?" Bless slowly sipped his beer. "The one in the paper?"

"Yeah . . ." Kenyatta's voice trailed off.

"So what happened with that?"

"With what?"

"Eve."

Kenyatta leaned in toward Bless on both elbows. The heavy smell of beer on his breath flooded Bless' nose. "She was a ho."

"A ho? The fuck-anything-movin'-type ho or a working ho?"

"A call girl. One of Collyn's chicks. This chick used to suck dick like you wouldn't believe."

"Damn."

"Yeah, and after a few paid dates I started getting inside this chick's head, hitting her with a buncha sweet bullshit, and the next thing I know she was fuckin' me for free."

"For free?"

"The fuck free." He sipped his beer. "I swear, a sincere-sounding 'I love you' does wonders for a desperate broad."

"Damn, sounds like you the man."

"Shiiiit, please." Kenyatta paused. Eve's bloody face filled his mind.

"Kenyatta?" Bless called. "You okay?"

"Yeah."

"Ai'ight, so finish the story. What happened to her?"

Kenyatta hesitated. "Damn if I know."

"You think she'll ever come back?"

"Nah . . . I don't think so."

TWENTY-TWO

Mehki had become Monday's reliable stress reliever. For the past three weeks she'd come again to enjoy his company, value his opinions, and the more she rekindled her friendship with him, laughed, and politicked with him, the more she realized that she was losing her desire for the public life. She wanted a change, and not one that required her to run away and become someone else. But one where she made choices for herself, and if she fucked up, she was the one affected by it, not an entire city.

Nevertheless, that didn't stop her heart from longing for Kenyatta. She felt obligated to him, as if she owed him something, and no matter how many chills shot up her spine as Mehki's moist and long tongue stroked her clit in precise movements, she never forgot she was Kenyatta's wife.

As they lay in a sixty-nine position Monday placed her hands on Mehki's knees and took him into her mouth. She'd tried at least a thousand times since they'd been fucking on a regular basis to give him a sweet head job, but his dick was simply too big to all fit in her mouth. But this time as she relaxed her throat and eased him in inch by inch, she was able to deep throat all of him.

"Monday," he licked her clit, "damn you sucking the hell outta this dick," he lifted his hips a bit so that she would be able to maintain his shaft between her heated lips.

After a few moments of blessing each other with head jobs and they were both ready to cum, their cell phones rang simultaneously.

They ignored them as Mehki said, "Smear it on my face," he moaned as a cell phone rang again. Mehki loved the smell of Monday's pussy and the way her cream felt against his skin. Grinding her hips, she rubbed her liquid all over his face, his eyes, his chin, his lips. Then she turned around and proceeded to kiss every sweet and sticky inch of him.

Afterward she opened her legs wide, and his body became one with hers. Monday gasped. Once again his size caught her off guard. He twirled her nipples. "If you keep riding my dick like this, in a minute you gon' be divorced."

"Hell, sometimes life needs change."

"Don't play with me."

"Who said that I was?" She took both her legs, wrapped them around his neck, and bounced on his dick, her ass caressing his entire shaft.

Her phone was ringing again. As soon as hers stopped, his started, almost as if they were in a competition.

Monday stopped midstroke. "Maybe we oughta get that."

"Fuck that." Mehki rolled her over so that he now lay on top. He took her legs and threw them on the side of his shoulder, then took his dick and came all over her ass. Mehki collapsed onto Monday's chest and rolled to the side of her. Monday stroked his cheek and said, "Why do I always have to be in the wet spot?"

Mehki chuckled. But before he could say anything, first one and then the other phone started ringing again. "Seriously," Monday said, "we need to get those." She reached for her purse while Mehki got out of bed and walked over to his dresser. As they each flipped their phones open and said hello concurrently, they hushed each other because they'd said hello too loudly.

"This is what the fuck I'm talking about." Kenyatta complained. "Where are you?" Monday's eyes scanned the room as she gathered the sheet over her breasts. She looked at Mehki's bare back and swinging dick as he walked across the room, holding the cell phone to his ear, and she said, "I'm where I wanna be."

"Monday, I promise you if you don't tell me where you are, whenever I see you it's gon' be a misunderstanding."

Tuning Kenyatta out, Monday listened to what Mehki was saying: "I need to get there now?" He tilted his head and looked at her apologetically. "I need to get there right now? All right, I'll be there."

Tuning back into her conversation, Monday said to Kenyatta, "Look, I don't have time for this shit."

"Why, 'cause you with some niggah right now? Don't think I haven't noticed that your ass been acting real foul."

"Look, Kenyatta, I do not have time. What do you want?"

"I need you to get your ass over here and act like the mayor's wife. Some shit just went down and I need you right now."

As Monday hung up Mehki looked her way. "I take it that was your husband."

"Damn, I do have one of those," Monday said sarcastically. "Glad you reminded me."

Mehki laughed. "That was Hudson. It looks like it's gray suit and pearls time again."

Monday's heart sank into her chest. She'd almost forgotten about that. "What the hell is going on?"

Mehki studied Monday's face before he spoke. "Eve Johnson's diary was found, and it implicated Kenyatta . . . as her lover."

"That was found a minute ago."

"I know, but apparently there were some pictures found too."

"Of them?"

"Yes."

"Together?"

"Yes, and apparently it's all over the media—reporters are calling City Hall, the mansion, and so on. It looks like we need to go to the mansion and see how this needs to be handled."

"Damn!" Monday exploded. "I'm sick of that shit! He's never been fuckin' faithful, and every time I turn around it's always some shit with this bitch! This same fuckin' bitch! I wish she would just fuckin' die! I'm sick of his cheating ass."

Mehki looked at Monday, taken aback. "So, you gon' kill the messenger?"

"No. But you don't know how it feels to have to go on TV in front of the world and be the dumbest ride-or-die bitch they've ever seen. Know what?" Monday pulled her knees to her chest. "I ain't goin' nowhere."

Mehki walked over to Monday, "You're welcome to stay here because I would love to come home to you in my bed. But you know I have to go. So make yourself at home. I'll be back in an hour, two hours tops, and we can chill." He grabbed a towel and headed into the bathroom.

Monday could hear the water beating against the tile in the shower as her back rested against the cool wall. She picked up the television remote. The midday news was of course talking about Kenyatta and the latest in the Eve Johnson scandal.

They showed pictures of Eve as well as previous press conferences and written statements where Kenyatta had said different things about the same situation.

Tears leaked from Monday's eyes. She no longer heard the commentator's voice; she could only see the pictures of herself, standing next to Kenyatta as he lied. She was tired of going back and forth, but he was still her husband.

Monday rose from the bed and grabbed her clothing. She opened the bathroom door, and Mehki was standing there, completely dressed in a gray suit. "You changed your mind?"

She pressed her lips against his and whispered, "I am the mayor's wife."

TWENTY-THREE

Monday walked in through the front door, leaving an ocean of reporters out by the security gate. When she pushed the door open to her bedroom, Kenyatta was standing there with Hudson, who was in Monday's walk-in closet, searching through her things.

"What the fuck are you doing?" Monday snapped as she watched Hudson pull her gray suit out of the closet and lay it on the bed.

"Don't worry about what she's doing!" Kenyatta snarled. "She's on her damn job, unlike your ass, which I called over an hour ago."

Monday ignored Kenyatta and instead turned to Hudson and said, "Why the hell are you in my closet?"

"I was just trying to help out."

"I don't need your damn help!"

"Are you ignoring me, Monday?" Kenyatta paced in disbelief. It was obvious that he was nervous, "Anyway, that isn't even important right now. What's important is that the authorities found some bogus-ass pictures and a diary that this bitch Eve wrote about me." He shook his head. "I can't keep doing this."

Hudson turned to him and said, "Kenyatta, we will rise above this. You cannot let this get you down."

Before Kenyatta could comment, there was a knock at the door, and they all turned around. It was Mehki. "You mind if I come in?"

"Yeah, come on," Kenyatta said. "We have to get our story straight before we go to the FBI."

Taken aback, Mehki said, "What are we going to see the FBI for? I thought we were just going to do a press conference."

"We have one scheduled right after this." Hudson stepped in. "This is about the best political move he can make. There have been a lot of things coming up and hitting us pretty hard, and in order to get past this, we need to have the mayor go and speak with the agents as if he has nothing to hide. The people will love that."

"Wait a minute—wait a minute," Mehki said. "What are you talking about, going down to the FBI? They haven't called to question him. They haven't even been here." Mehki turned to Kenyatta. "And what are you going to say to the FBI?"

"Look, I have to clear my name. Reporters have been calling me all day." He turned to look at Monday, thinking of how long he'd been trying to get in touch with her. "And all of this shit is just becoming a little too much."

"That's why," Hudson said, "we're going down to the FBI for him to voluntarily make a statement, so this way they will think he has nothing to hide. We will regain the people's trust, and we can move on."

Mehki looked at Hudson strangely. "As your attorney," he said to Kenyatta, "I don't advise you to do that. I mean, come on. We all are attorneys here, so certainly someone understands where I'm coming from. Going down to the FBI makes absolutely no sense. What are you going to go down there for? To perjure yourself?"

"No one said anything about perjury," Hudson insisted. "This is not about perjury. This is about political positioning."

"No, this is not about political positioning," Mehki snapped, "this is about committing a federal crime! Furthermore, it was a diary. You haven't even seen it nor do you know what it says. And you don't even know if you are in those photos. But you are going to break-dance down to the FBI's office, and for what? You're going to make a statement for what reason? Trust me—if they want you, they will find you. You don't have to look for them!"

Hudson interrupted him and said sternly to Kenyatta, "As your chief of staff, I know that we have the ability to rise above this and regain the people's trust. And in order to regain their trust we have to show that we have nothing to hide. Besides, being mayor is just a stepping-stone. Kenyatta has the talent and the leadership ability to go all the way to the top."

"That's what I'm talking about," Kenyatta interjected.

Monday waved, "Kenyatta do you hear how ridiculous you sound?"

"What the hell!" Kenyatta snapped. "And you supposed to be my wife? And every time I need you to support me, you always off on some bullshit. Let me tell you something, I am a great mayor."

"Yes you are," Hudson chimed in.

"I proposed to cut property taxes, I raised the school budget, built more houses in the poor areas, opened more job programs, more local parks, free camps, and all sorts of shit. I paid my dues and I'm not gon' let some dead bitch—"

Monday shook her head, there it was again.

"Fuck up everything," Kenyatta continued, "I worked hard for."

"Exactly." Hudson smiled in admiration, "Exactly."

• • •

As they walked into the federal building Hudson held her cell phone to her ear. "Everything has been arranged," she said to Kenyatta. "We just need to ask for Agent Jones and Agent West in the Missing Persons Squad."

They walked into the interrogation room, where the agents were already sitting. Everyone shook hands and then took their seats.

"Thank you for coming down here," Agent Jones said. "We sincerely appreciate it. And we just want you to know that everything we say in this room will be recorded."

"Okay," Kenyatta said, clearing his throat. "That's not a problem. I just came down here so that I can clear my name." He cleared his throat again and his voice began to sound mechanical. "I come humbly before you to extend my sympathy to the family of this missing person, Eve, because a man such as myself is always willing to get the truth out there. I just want to address some things that have been in the media, especially since I'm such a stand-up person and have nothing to hide. And I wanted to address some of the bullshit that ho wrote about me."

Mehki cleared his throat and placed his hand on Kenyatta's shoulder. "What I meant was," Kenyatta said, "the diary is some bull— some nonsense. And the pictures. I'm sure they aren't of me." The FBI agent slid the pictures to Kenyatta. . They were of him and Eve entering a hotel lobby. "That could've been at a political event." They slid him another photo of them kissing. Kenyatta cleared his throat, "Gentlemen, I bid you farewell."

He rose from his seat, but Agent Jones said, "Excuse me, Mayor, but we just want to ask you a few more questions if you don't mind."

"Perhaps we should cut this short," Mehki said.

"We won't be long, Counselor." Agent Jones insisted, "surely such a great mayor doesn't mind helping us to clear things up."

"No." Kenyatta sat back down. "Not at all."

"Well," Agent Jones said, "we appreciate you coming down here and taking time from your busy schedule. You know, being humble and all."

"Excuse me." Kenyatta looked around the room. "Are you mocking me?" Mehki placed his hand back on Kenyatta's shoulder.

"No sir," the agent went on. "We would never do such a thing. We just wanted you to answer a few things and then you may go."

"Ai'ight, go ahead . . . I mean, proceed."

"Thank you, Mayor Smith. So did you or did you not have an affair with Eve Johnson?"

"I've already addressed that issue."

"Okay, sir, do you know a retired cop by the name of Tracy Robinson?"

Kenyatta blinked and his heart thundered in his chest. "No."

Monday's palms began to sweat, there was that name again.

"Okay, so," the agent continued, "let me ask you this. Did you have an affair with Collyn Bazemore?"

Monday's neck jerked. Collyn's was the last name she expected to hear. Scared of what might come from the agent's mouth next, she started biting her bottom lip.

"Collyn?" Kenyatta said, taken aback. "Hell no."

"Okay, uh . . . what about Taryn. Taryn Bazemore?"

"Taryn?" Kenyatta hesitated. "No."

"Okay, so what about Geneva Thompson?"

"Geneva Thompson," Kenyatta said distantly. "Never heard of her."

The agents looked at Monday and then back at each other.

"I don't know what motherfuckin' game you playin'," Kenyatta spat, "but this interview is over with."

Acting as if he'd never said a word, they continued on. "And what about Hudson James?"

The entire room looked at Hudson as Monday gasped.

Instantly Kenyatta exploded. "How the fuck y'all gon' ask me some shit like that in front of my wife? Disrespecting me and shit! Y'all motherfuckers don't know Kenyatta Smith."

"Ooo-kay," Mehki said, "let's go, ladies." He grabbed Kenyatta by the arm. "We need to leave now."

"Nah, nah!" Kenyatta snatched the buttons open on his double-breasted suit jacket.

Mehki's grip tightened on him. "Let's go now!" he said sternly as he shoved the mayor through the door.

TWENTY-FOUR

The sea of cameras flashed in Monday's eyes once again as she stood dressed in her press conference uniform: gray skirt, matching jacket, and pearls. She was at the podium beside Kenyatta, who cleared his throat. The crowd quieted down.

He stood with his back straight, looking somber and feeling sorry for himself that he'd been caught in yet another lie. He looked directly into the camera and began to speak. "Good evening. I come humbly before you as not only the mayor of our great city but also as a man who comes to say I'm sorry. I'm sorry to all of you who have been hurt by the recent allegations of me being involved with Eve Johnson . . ."

He turned to Monday. She'd missed her cue to squeeze

his hand; seeing that she hadn't picked up on it, Kenyatta continued on. "I have apologized to my wife for the hurt that I have caused our marriage. But that in no way affects my ability to lead this city. However, there seems to be a vendetta against me, because now very private and personal things that have gone on between my wife and myself have come out in the paper." Again Monday missed her cue. Kenyatta looked at her, and to the public he seemed to have a look of sorrow on his face, one of apology that he'd hurt her. Only Monday knew that the look indicated that it would be on this afternoon.

"So, my great city, I am here to deal with the series of articles and reports that have accused me of being involved in an adulterous relationship with Eve Johnson. And even if that were true it has nothing to do with my ability to run this city. I want you to know that you are all that matters, so I humbly apologize to you for the pain that these allegations may have caused."

Monday started unbuttoning her gray jacket.

Her eyes watered as she grew exhausted of standing in this spot and standing behind him every time he lied, making her look like a damn fool to everybody here and across the world. This had gone far beyond what she'd ever thought she would accept in life. So while the cameras were rolling and he was remixing the truth to fit the last lie he told, she simply walked out and left Kenyatta there alone.

"Monday." Mehki walked up swiftly behind her. "Where are you going?"

"I need to leave. I can't fuckin' breathe in here."

"But where are you going?"

"I don't know, but I have to get out of here." Tears dripped down her face. She was sick and tired of being sick and tired.

"Come here." He pulled her to his chest. "I'll take you home."

Noticing a sea of reporters up ahead, Mehki took her hand, walked with her to his car, and they left.

TWENTY-FIVE

Collyn sat Indian style on her couch with a bowl of popcorn in her hand, watching the mayor's news conference. She, like everyone else, couldn't believe that Monday had actually walked off the stage and left Kenyatta standing there. "It's about damn time!" She smiled. "Taryn," she yelled, "Bless!.Come here and see this shit."

Taryn ran into the living room with the baby swinging on her hip. "You have got to see this." Collyn laughed as Bless sat down on the floor between her legs.

"What happened?" he asked.

"Look," she said, grabbing the remote and replaying the scene on the DVR. They all watched Monday walk off the stage, leaving Kenyatta standing there looking like a fool.

Taryn started laughing. In fact, she laughed so hard that tears fell from her eyes and her shoulders shook.

"You better stop laughing at your baby's daddy." Collyn wiped tears of hilarity from her eyes.

Bless glanced over at Taryn. "Wait a minute. Nah, she's not really his daughter, is she? That was a joke?"

"Shit," Collyn said. "It was a joke, but two years and a late child support check later, it ain't funny."

"Damn." Bless turned to Collyn. "Did he fuck you too?"

She mushed him on the side of the head. "Niggah, I wouldn't dare fuck that dirty-dick motherfucker."

"Excuse you," Taryn snapped.

"Oh, don't be mad, Taryn," Collyn snickered as she and Bless fell against the back of the couch, laughing. "Don't be mad."

TWENTY-SIX

Collyn's phone rang as Bless was in midstroke. He looked at Collyn. "You know I'm not stopping, right?"

"Wait, baby." Her breasts bounced in the air. "Let me get it. It's security—something could be wrong."

"Go 'head," he insisted. "You can talk; I don't have to say anything all I have to do is stroke."

Collyn picked up the phone as Bless continued. Doing her best to keep the pleasure from trembling her voice, she said, "Yes?"

"Good evening, Ms. Bazemore. Mrs. Smith is here to see you."

Collyn hesitated and looked at Bless. She placed her hand over the receiver and said, "Monday's downstairs."

"Dayum."

"Don't be like that."

Holding his head down and shaking it, he said, "What do you think she wants?"

"I don't know."

Bless rolled to the side and said, "Well, I think you need to find out."

Collyn returned her attention to the phone and said to Adam, "Thank you, and please send her up." Collyn slipped out of bed, wrapped her robe around her, and headed to the front door. She opened it and Monday stood there, her face streaked with running mascara and her clothes tousled. "What happened to you? Kenyatta caught your ass after you walked off TV?"

Monday walked toward her and into the apartment. "Do I look like I'm laughing? And furthermore, I'm just gon' get to the point: are you fucking Kenyatta?"

Collyn chuckled. "What?"

"You heard me! Are you fucking my husband? Is Taryn still fucking my husband? What the fuck is really going on here?"

"What the hell are you talking about? Is this a damn joke?"

"Do I look funny to you?"

"You don't wanna know what you look like to me. And furthermore, I've already had a conversation with you about rolling up on me and acting crazy. Now, if you have something you want to say, you need to hurry up and say it, because I have some things to do with a real man."

Monday stood still and studied Collyn's face, wondering if she should believe her or not. Looking at her and determining that she was telling the truth, Monday sighed, "I didn't want to believe it . . ." Monday broke down into tears, "but I think Kenyatta may have killed Eve."

Collyn sat down on the couch as Monday cried her heart out about everything that had been going on. "The FBI saying one thing, Kenyatta saying another thing. I just feel like I'm going crazy."

Collyn said, "What do you mean, the FBI?"

"Kenyatta involved them. He insisted we go down there today, and when we got there it blew up in his face. They were insinuating all kinds of shit. I found out that Tracy is not a working girl."

"How'd you find that out?"

"They were naming names and said that Tracy was an ex-cop. They even asked if Kenyatta was sleeping with you, if he was sleeping with Taryn, and they even called me by Geneva. Nobody knows me by Geneva!"

Collyn was confused. "Calling names? What were they looking for? And why would Kenyatta voluntarily go to see the FBI?"

"He went to answer questions about Eve Johnson's diary and some pictures they found."

"Pictures? Questions? What questions?" Collyn asked, thinking about her recent visit to the FBI and hoping that her lies wouldn't come back to haunt her. "What exactly did Kenyatta say? Did he admit to anything?"

Monday looked at Collyn, surprised. "Now, you know Kenyatta's ass ain't admitting shit. Not even that he or somebody he knows killed this bitch."

Collyn sighed with relief. "What about the pictures?"

"They were of him and Eve . . . kissing." Monday's voice drifted.

"Damn . . . so tell me from the beginning what exactly happened?"

Monday recapped for Collyn all of the events that had taken place. Once she was done, Collyn looked at Monday and said, "So what are you going to do?"

"Why does everybody keep asking me that? I don't know. I really don't know."

Collyn chuckled a bit. "Maybe if you change your name to Next Week Friday it'll help you out a bit."

"Yeah," Monday said, Collyn failing to cheer her up, "maybe."

TWENTY-SEVEN

Monday hadn't come home last night and Kenyatta had yet to deal with her the way he needed to for embarrassing him. If it weren't for the meeting with the City Council he was on his way to, he'd be searching all over New York for this bitch.

Kenyatta walked down the corridor to the City Council chamber, his leather briefcase in his hand. Given the most recent events in his life and how everything seemed to be spinning out of control, it was hard for him to keep a blank face and maintain his confidence.

He pushed open the double doors to the packed room. "Good morning, Council." Kenyatta nodded, his voice displaying a tone of self-assurance. He and Hudson took their seats behind the microphones on the long table that faced the members of the City Council.

Thomas Askew, the Council Speaker, called the meeting to order. After a few moments of confirming everyone's attendance, the Council leader began to speak.

"Mayor Smith," Thomas said as he pushed his glasses up the bridge of his nose, "we've called this special meeting to discuss with you the most recent scandals surrounding your personal life and the lawsuit by the ex-city employee as well as the allegation of misappropriation of city funds, all of which have stunned the city and shaken its trust in our local government. We believe that it would be best for the people of New York City if you were to resign."

Kenyatta sat in his chair paralyzed. His political career passed before him. He thought about how he was groomed for politics as a child, seeing his father campaign and fight for what he believed was right, his mother at her husband's side. He thought about how no one knew the difficulty, yet there was a strong sense of pride that came along with starting from the bottom and working his way up, stopping for a brief moment at being mayor and then proceeding on. New York was simply a layover; Washington, D.C., was the destination.

And here these fifty-one out-of-touch motherfuckers, who couldn't run the city without him, thought that because they got together and decided they wanted a new mayor, he should simply tuck his tail between his legs and leave? Please. Fuck them. As far as Kenyatta was concerned, they could kiss his black ass.

Kenyatta stood up from his chair, grabbed his briefcase, and said, "I'm going back to work."

"Excuse me, Mayor," Thomas said, astonished at Kenyatta's response. "Do you understand the seriousness of this? You're in the paper every day—"

"That's not your problem."

"I beg your pardon. That is very much our problem. Let's be for real here. You've embarrassed the city beyond belief."

Hudson stood up. "Perhaps we should cool off and discuss this later."

"I'm not discussing shit," Kenyatta snapped. "Did you know about this?" Before Hudson could respond, he continued, "This meeting is adjourned."

The room became filled with steady buzzing as everyone looked at Kenyatta in disbelief.

"Mayor Smith!" Thomas said, infuriated. "We have had enough."

"I'm not resigning. Do not call me here to discuss anything unless it has to do with the city." And he stormed out.

Hudson followed Kenyatta back to his office. "Kenyatta, look, we can rise above this!"

"Know what?" He swiveled around and looked her directly in the face. "If you wish to proceed with a prosperous political career, you'll get the fuck out my face! Now rise above that!" He walked her roughly to the door, practically pushed her across the threshold, and slammed the door in her face.

After a few minutes of talking himself into calming down, Kenyatta called Tracy. "Man look, I need to hear something, please." Kenyatta begged.

"No new leads on Eve," Tracy responded. "But I do have that information you asked for on Geneva Thompson."

TWENTY-EIGHT

Kenyatta sat in the blue-striped parlor. Subdued darkness bathed the room as he lay back in the velvet Queen Anne wing chair, watching the single stream of light ease into the foyer as Monday carefully opened the front door.

"Where've you been, Monday?" Kenyatta's voice cut through the darkness.

Monday jumped.

"Where've you been?" Kenyatta asked.

"Why"—she spoke slowly—"are you sitting in the dark?"

"I've been trying to reach you. Where've you been?"

"I, um . . ." She paused. "I had some thinking to do."

"Like what?"

Monday's eyes scanned what little she could see of him, "Why?"

"Answer my question."

"I was just out thinking."

Dead silence.

"Let's try this again." Kenyatta stood to his feet. "Where were you?"

"Shopping." Another lie. She hoped he didn't catch the tremble in her voice. Her plan was to get her things and leave. No hard feelings, no second guesses, just a set of goodbyes that were long overdue. Monday began to feel uneasy. "Where's the staff?"

"I gave them the night off."

Kenyatta walked over and closed the parlor's double doors. He then sat back in the wing chair and pulled her between his legs. "I need you to be honest." Though it was a statement, his tone reflected a warning.

"About what?" Monday's hands trembled between his. "I don't like this shit." She stepped back. "What is all this darkness and the staff being given the night off really about? I know we haven't discussed me walking out on the press conference. But . . . I just—"

Kenyatta stood up and pulled her back to him. "You see the newspaper today?"

"No." Her heart dropped. "Why?"

"You've been out all day and you haven't seen the paper?"

"No." She tried to back away again and he tightened his hold on her waist.

"Stop moving." He gave her another warning.

She complied.

"Any reporters run after you while you were out?"

"Reporters?" She squinted. "Why, what happened now?"

"The City Council asked me to step down."

"What?"

"Yeah, but that's only half of what fucked me up today." He looked at her. "So you were out in public and nothing? No one, not even one person on the street, stopped you?"

"Would you just tell me what happened? You're scaring me!"

"You scared of me now? Of me? Since when that shit happen?"

"I'ma go upstairs."

"No, you will stand right here. Now, I need to understand how you've been out in public all day shopping and no one approached you. No reporters, no one?"

"What did I just say? And why are you badgering me about this?"

"Because you weren't out in the street! You're lying and you've been lying ever since I met you."

"What are you talking about?"

"Who is Geneva Thompson?"

Monday stepped back. This was the second time in a week she'd heard the same question, and this time, just like the last, she felt sliced down the middle of her chest.

Monday's mind clouded with a million memories at once as she tried to figure out what had gone on today that fucking Mehki had stopped her from finding out. "Where is all of this coming from?" she asked.

No answer.

Monday stared at him. Though the room was dark, her eyes had long since adjusted. Now she could see into his face, and she could tell by his glare that he knew who Geneva Thompson really was.

She started to tell him that the whore was dead, buried at birth when her mother left her with a father who started out fine but ended up not giving a fuck.

"Why are you asking me this?" she asked as her heart raced.

"Were you a whore bitch?" His words were like stab wounds.

"It wasn't like that. And don't call me a bitch!" She started to back away, tears streaming down her face.

"Is that a yes?"

She walked backward and he came toward her.

"I didn't have anybody, Kenyatta." Tears streamed from her eyes.

"Is that a yes?" They continued to walk.

"My mother left me. And the only thing I have of her is the reflection of my face."

"So it's yes?"

"And my father . . . he tried, but once he got married that was it for me. My grandmother's name was Monday and she loved me. And that's what I wanted. I wanted to be loved. I wanted to be accepted. I wanted to be something, anything, just someone to somebody—"

"A fuckin' whore?"

"I had no money and I wanted to go to college—to law school. I needed to be someone other than a poor-ass country girl with nothing but clay dirt under her feet. I needed to become someone else, and I was too scared of suicide, so I had to kill myself another way!"

"What the fuck are you talking about?" he screamed in her face. She took another step away and banged the back of her head on the wall.

"I was Geneva Thompson."

The air froze. Kenyatta felt like someone was pounding organ keys in his head. He couldn't move. He thought about what she'd told him over the years: that her parents had died in a tragic accident, and with the exception of a cousin she kept in touch with in Georgia, she had no one.

And here he'd thought he could save her and mold her to be not only the wife he'd wanted but the one his father, who was a state senator, had told him he would need.

Here he'd thought he'd found his diamond in the rough. She was beautiful, smart, and fulfilling, and she catered to his every need. There was no drama, no criminal, emotional, or any other type of come-back-to-haunt-them-later background, or so he'd thought. She had everyone fooled. They all thought she was a good girl, someone special on his team, who insisted that instead of accepting political favors from his family, he work his way to the top and pull himself up by his bootstraps. This was why he'd never left her. Despite the other women having his babies, despite their physical ability to give him what she hadn't, he loved her—because she loved him, flaws and all.

Now here he stood, betrayal rocking him to the core of his being, looking at this bitch cry as if her life had been stolen, when he was the one who'd been robbed without a gun.

"And to think," Kenyatta sneered, "that every motherfuckin' body always felt sorry for yo' hookin' ass when something I did jumped off, not knowing that all along it's really been you playing the shit outta me!"

Kenyatta squinted. The light that snuck in through the sliver of space beneath the door blinded him as he bit down on his bottom lip and smacked Monday so hard she stumbled before falling to her ass and skidding across the floor. "I been married to a fuckin' whore for ten years?" He spat in disbelief. "Ten years you've been lying to me? You said your parents were dead—"

"They are dead." She held the side of her face, which now was swollen and showed the imprint of his hand.

"You said you had one cousin you kept in touch with—"

"I do!"

"But nowhere in all that did you ever say you were a whore!"

Silence.

"Is this why you don't have any friends, bitch? You ain't shit! A fuckin' whore! So tell me, Geneva, what's your red light special?" He lifted her by the neck and pressed her into the wall. "A half-and-half?" He ripped her blouse open. The shearing of the material sizzled through the room. "A full body or some ass?"

She pushed him and yelled, "What about all the shit you've done to me? I would've never done any of that to you!"

"Did I give you permission to speak, Geneva?" He mushed her across the face, causing her neck to jerk back.

"Stop it!" Monday tearfully cried, pushing him in the chest again. "What the fuck are you doing?"

"Ain't no motherfuckin' stop, Jah-nee-va! What I need to pay you? How much you charge?" He reached in his pocket, pulled out a wad of money, and tossed it like confetti into her face.

"Get the fuck off of me, Kenyatta!" His body weight had never felt so heavy pressed against her.

Ignoring her demand, Kenyatta unzipped his pants. "What you telling me to stop for? That's at least a thousand dollars— it should get me an hour!"

"I'm not a fuckin' whore!"

"You a low-down dirty slut, bitch." He backhanded her. "I got a good mind to make you bend to your knees and suck my dick!"

Monday tried to fight against his embrace, but she was no match for him. "I swear to God, if you don't get offa me I'ma call—"

Kenyatta gave her half a grin and let out a sinister laugh. "You gon' call who? The cops? I run them motherfuckers, or did you forget? You may as well drop all that damsel-in-distress bullshit and recognize you my bottom bitch and I'm your motherfuckin' pimp!" He tore her skirt and roughly pulled it off her. "Is this why you like me to fuck you so rough? Is this why I can fuck you any way I want to, because underneath all of this shit"—he ripped her panties off in one sweep— "you turning tricks?"

Tears streamed down Monday's face and ran like a waterfall into the corners of her mouth. Her punches into his chest were no match for the way he was gripping her neck and squeezing the sides.

Monday continued to scream, her words muffled by the tight grip around her throat. She wildly shook her head, but she wasn't sure if he wasn't paying attention or he simply didn't give a fuck.

"Didn't I just pay you for this, Geneva? Didn't I?" He yanked her hair and pushed her face toward his. "Didn't I?"

Monday's screams had faded into silent and painful tears.

"Say yes!" He forcibly made her head nod. "Say yes." He forced her to nod again. "That's what the fuck I thought, so don't tell me no!" Kenyatta stared into Monday's eyes. He could feel her trembling in his arms. He hated that thoughts of her fucking another niggah blinded him.

"Please stop," Monday tearfully whispered. "Please. I'm sorry . . . I am . . . but please . . ." Her whispers were so low that they barely rose above the iron lump in her throat.

Kenyatta let Monday's neck go and started walking away. He was out of his mind and knew he needed to leave before he did something they both regretted.

Monday's chest heaved as she stood with her tattered blouse hanging and her hip bruised from the force of Kenyatta ripping her underwear off. She watched him walk backward across the room, twist the knob on the double doors, and head off into the light that streamed down the foyer.

TWENTY-NINE

It was a last-minute trip to the Bahamas they'd planned at Bless' insistence. Collyn had been sick off and on for the last two weeks and he thought maybe getting away would make her feel better. So they chartered a plane and flew to Paradise Island for an overnight getaway.

Along with the tropical sun blazing, Collyn awoke dripping wet this morning with Bless' warm tongue resting on her clit. "Good morning," he said, looking into her eyes as she lay in the center of the beach bungalow's wooden bed. The net canopy draped from the ceiling to the bamboo floor.

Bless placed his thumb on her clit and sucked her inner thigh. Realigning his lips with her slit, he licked the length of her pussy.

"Okay." She arched her back, unable to fight off the chilling sensation. "You gotta li'l fetish going on? What's next—you gon' blindfold me or some shit?"

"Ai'ight, cool. You don't want it, I'll stop." And Bless rolled over, his defined body making an imprint in the Bragada mattress as the fine woven-bamboo fabric of the sheets massaged his tight and naked ass. He looked at his dick. "She don't want none." He started stroking it. "But she don't know." He looked at his hands. "We make a perfect couple."

Collyn could still feel the sensation of his tongue. "Why did you stop?" She pushed on his shoulder. "Bless—"

"What?" He cupped his shaft, his hard-on looking like a sweet log of fudge to her eyes and making her mouth water, "What's the problem? Since I'm sick you don't get no dick."

"Baby"—she climbed between his legs—"don't be mad. I was just playing."

"You play too much." He watched her slide down his chest and suck the fingers he cupped his dick with.

"My clit is throbbing."

"That pussy nice and wet, ain't it?"

"Mmm-hmmm," she moaned. Collyn leaned forward and stuck her index finger into her pussy and then into his mouth. "Taste it. Ain't it good?"

"Nah." He sucked her finger. "It's ai'ight."

Collyn couldn't help laughing. "My baby mad?"

"Pissed the fuck off."

"Aw." She slid down his stomach and took him into her mouth.

"You accept my apology, baby?"

"Yes." He fucked her mouth. "Oh yes."

After pleasuring each other for the next hour, they awoke to Collyn's phone ringing. "No calls," Bless said, taking her phone so the call would go to voice mail.

"But suppose something important has come up and it's Taryn?"

"Collyn, damn, we're only gone for a day. We'll be back tomorrow."

"I guess, Bless."

• • •

After making love for most of the day, Bless and Collyn dressed in leisure outfits. He had on a pair of long black linen shorts, matching black leather flip-flops, and a sleeveless white tee, while she wore a white linen tennis dress and nothing on her feet. They walked along the private beach and played tag, she rode on his back, and they laughed like they'd never laughed before in their lives.

"Yo," Bless said, "Let's go over the bridge to Nassau and hang out."

"Blessing," Collyn whined as she lay back on the bed, feeling nauseous again, "maybe tomorrow."

"We'll be back home tomorrow. Now come on we came to have some fun."

Collyn turned over and smiled at him. Whenever she looked directly in his face she could never deny him. "All right," she gave in, "but only for a little while."

"Straight, and I got the perfect spot."

• • •

"What kinda . . . place is this?" Collyn looked around at the local pool hall where the concrete walls were painted Carribean turquoise and trimmed in pink. There were windows with no frames or screens, a lime green painted bar with a gold marble top, and a DJ who was jamming just as hard to the music he played as the people on the packed dance floor. A Shabba Ranks throwback sizzled through the tight concrete slab they were partying on. Most of the people in here were natives, and whoever wasn't drinking was doing a "dutty whine" on the dance floor.

"Don't even try and act like you ain't down wit' the get down. Especially not when that fat ass," he slapped her on it, "is screaming West Indian." Bless kissed Collyn on the lips and pulled her to the center of the floor. "Come on beautiful, dance with me."

Collyn smiled; although she wanted to tell him to take her back to bed, didn't want to ruin his time, especially since the trip was done for her benefit. So she threw her hips in motion and began to dance with him like nobody's business.

After they finished dancing Collyn asked Bless, "Do you play pool?"

"Nah . . .," he playfully mushed her, "I whups ass at pool."

Collyn twisted her lips, "Niggah, please."

"So what, you wanna get embarrassed?"

Collyn laughed, "I got fifty dollars that says I won't."

"And it better not be no Bahamian money either."

"Whatever." Collyn said as they walked over to the pool table in the dimly lit far corner.

"Rack the balls," Collyn said.

Bless shot her a look, "Ai'ight."

She winked her eye, "You know I can't hit it that good, can you show me how to knock the balls in the socket?"

"Now you fucking with me. Keep it up and I'ma have a trick for your ass." Bless chalked two sticks and handed her one, "This is a grown man's game anyway."

"Whatever," Collyn said as she broke the first shot and missed.

"My point exactly." He walked up behind her, leaned his chest on her back, and took a shot. The ball went in the pocket, and as he quickly went to take another shot, bending over her again, she started gyrating her ass onto his shaft, causing him to miss his shot.

"I'm warning you to stop." He said, as his dick turned to iron.

"What's wrong?" she positioned herself for a shot and Bless rubbed his hands along her thighs.

She looked over her shoulder, "Play fair, Bless."

Bless laughed, "Don't be scared, take a shot." He ran his hands up her skirt and pulled at the sides of her panties. "Let me take 'em off."

"Would you stop?"

"Come on, ain't nobody gon' see." He started pulling them down her thighs, over her knees, and she quickly and quietly stepped out of them. Bless slipped them into his pocket and said, "Take a shot." He rotated two fingers in.

"Bless," she dropped her stick on the table and knocked three balls from their place.

"My turn." He took a shot. "We gon' dead this early, you gon' learn not to play with me."

"What, you think I still can't win?" She grinded against him.

Bless handed her the stick, "Take a shot."

"It's your turn," she said.

"Nah," he insisted, "go ahead."

Collyn took the stick from his hands, stood on her tiptoes, took a shot, and when she came back down, Bless rubbed the head of his dick between her pussy lips, causing her to tilt forward. "Bless—"

"What's the problem?" He pushed his dick all the way in and she screamed.

"Would you shut the fuck up?" He covered her mouth. "How come every time we fuck you gotta be all loud and shit? Chill."

Collyn lifted her eyes and smiled at a few onlookers. "People are looking, Bless" she said tight-lipped.

He stroked, "Fuck them, they don't know what we're doing. It's dark in here and with my black ass they can't see shit but my teeth." He bit her on the neck, stroked twice, and took a shot. "Move along with me." He reached forward and took three shots, each time moving into her pussy as deep as he could.

Collyn knew at any minute she was due to cum. His lusciousness filled her up tremendously and all of his strokes were driven with perfection. Collyn fought like hell to keep her eyes open, forcing herself to remember where she was. But as he pumped in and out of her, and the reggae music provided a backdrop to his erotic beat, she was forced to give up the fight. So she closed her eyes, he bit her on the side of her neck, and they both rocked each other into oblivion.

THIRTY

"I need to stop by the gallery on the way home," Collyn said as they stepped off the chartered jet at LaGuardia Airport and into the town car.

"For what?" Bless asked, concerned about how tired she looked. "You need to go home and get in bed."

"I will, but after I go to the gallery. I need to pick up my mail, see if any orders have come in, things like that."

Reluctantly Bless agreed. "You know I really want you to go home, but ai'ight, we can stop by so you can handle your business. But we're not staying for long. I'm sure Taryn can hold down the fort." Bless kissed Collyn on her warm forehead and then informed the driver of their stop. Afterward he joined her in the backseat, where she laid down and placed her head in his lap.

Forty-five minutes of rush-hour traffic later, they pulled up in front of the gallery. Collyn noticed something different, but at that moment she couldn't figure out what had changed.

After the driver opened the door, she and Bless slid out of the car, stood in front of the gallery window, and stared. For a brief moment she wondered where were the hand-carved ivory African statues and hand-blown French vases that usually sat in the window. She pushed the door, noticing nothing was locked, and that's when it clicked: she'd been hit. Everything in the gallery that wasn't broken was missing.

Collyn turned to look at Bless, whose feet crushed broken glass as he walked over to where she was. Collyn rubbed her temples, feeling as if at any moment her head were going to explode.

"Collyn—" Bless' voice revealing that he was also in shock.

She didn't answer. Instead, she ignored him and walked to her office. She stood in the doorway. Her once-sleek modern-design space looked as if a whirlwind had come through. Her eyes swept to her desk. Her computer was missing, and her file cabinets were gone. She walked over to her desk and checked her drawers. Her ledger was gone.

Her head started to spin, "Collyn—" Bless called again.

She spun around. "What the fuck?" she screamed.

Before he could answer, Taryn rushed in. "Collyn, I've been trying to reach you since yesterday! Where were you?"

Collyn ignored her question and instead said, "What the fuck happened here?"

"The goddamn FBI came up in here and raided the motherfucker. And I just got back from being dragged down in handcuffs for fucking questioning."

"The FBI?" Collyn interjected. "What the fuck did they do this shit for?"

"They raided the place and took every goddamn thing!"

"FBI?" Bless echoed. "What?"

"I'm so sick of these motherfuckers fucking with me behind that goddamn Kenyatta!"

"And they came looking for you. They have a warrant for your arrest!" Taryn went on. "Have you been home? I'm sure they've been there."

"When did this happen?" Bless asked.

"They busted up in here last night!" Taryn screamed.

"What did they say?" Bless asked. "Did they serve you with a search warrant?"

"Yes." She handed him a copy of the warrant.

Collyn felt dizzy. She wavered back and forth before sitting down in the chair, tears slipping from her eyes. "I don't fuckin' believe this!" She stared at Bless. "I told you turning the phones off was a bad fuckin' idea."

"Look, let me take care of this. Taryn, take her home," he said.

"I'm not going home. I'm not some damn damsel in distress—this is my business!"

"I understand that, but you need to go home." He held the warrant in his hand, "And let me handle this." He looked at Taryn. "Take her home. I'll meet you there."

• • •

Special Agent Blessing Shields was fucked up. Never had he been in love like this, and without warning the shit had to end. It was as if he had forgotten about the undercover investigation he was assigned to. He'd gotten sidetracked from his original investigation of misappropriation of city funds and fraud. And though he was prepared to close in on Kenyatta, he should have been preparing himself for this day, when he'd have to tell Collyn he was an agent and that everything about them was a lie, except for how much he loved her.

"What the hell is this?" He pushed the door open to the conference room, where his supervisor, Agent Jones, Agent West, the prosecutor, and a few other people from the Missing Persons Squad were sitting. He slammed the warrant on the table, rattling the Styrofoam cups of coffee and tins of peppermints. "Why the hell would you do some shit like that to her?"

Cigarette smoke traveled to the ceiling as they all looked at him in shock.

"Agent Shields, I think you need to get a hold of yourself," said the agent in charge, Pamela Smiley, Bless' supervisor. "And in five minutes meet me in my office. Until then you are to be excused."

Bless picked up the warrant off the table, looked at everyone awkwardly, and backed out the room.

Fifteen minutes later, Agent Smiley strolled into her office, where Bless sat waiting for her. She closed the door behind her and walked over to her desk. She looked him in the eyes and said, "Have you calmed down now?"

Bless attempted to give her an answer, yet before he could speak she carried on. "What the hell is wrong with you?"

"I realize I got a little out of line."

"A little out of line? You've been out of line for the last few months. I think you've forgotten what you were assigned to do, Special Agent Blessing Shields. You were supposed to be investigating Mayor Kenyatta Smith, not frolicking in the Bahamas with some high-priced madam!"

Bless sat back in his chair and sighed while his superior continued. "Man, Smith has been in the news every goddamn day, and where have you been? Agent Jones and Agent West seemed to have been doing your job. Can you explain that to me?"

"I've been doing my job, but I was not informed that a raid was going to happen at her place of business."

"Well, you might have been informed if you'd kept your

phone on. Now look." She arched her eyebrows. "Collyn Baze-more is the Missing Persons Squad's problem, not ours. You are investigating Mayor Kenyatta Smith. Now the Missing Persons Squad is looking for her. And if you know where she is, then perhaps you need to go and talk to her about turning herself in."

"For what?"

"Number one, for perjury. Our department is now merging this investigation with the Missing Persons Squad, since we are now both investigating Mayor Kenyatta Smith. And who knows, maybe we'll be able to get her some type of deal if she's willing to talk and give us what we want on the mayor."

Bless rubbed the back of his hand over his face as he realized that this was out of his control. Lowering his hand and looking at his superior, he said, "So what kind of deal are we talking about?"

TO THIS

THIRTY-ONE

Snow fell from the late winter sky as Bless sat in the middle of Collyn's stark white sectional amidst the pale light of the setting sun.

He slid his hands in the side pockets of his black hoodie and tossed his head back. He wondered how he'd gotten to this place, this space, where his heart sat at the base of his throat, with its strings dancing in his mouth. He never thought he'd feel an iron fist grooving on his tongue. Nonetheless, it was there and he was here, waiting to tell the woman he'd fallen for that loving her had never been a part of the plan.

He hoped that when he told her the truth, she would accept it like a chick on the soap operas or an evening drama, where all that mattered was love despite how it manifested itself. But he knew he didn't have that type of woman. He knew Collyn would flip, cuss, punch, and then when all was said and done she would stop midswing and tell him to leave. Besides, this was life and shit wasn't scripted— nobody in her right mind would ride off into the sunset with a lying-ass knight and his gleaming FBI shield. So . . . it was what it was.

After a few moments of deafening silence, Bless heard Collyn's keys jingling in the lock. Tears threatened to fill his eyes as knots twisted in his back. The thought of their love transforming to despair made him sick to his stomach, so he pressed his elbows into his knees, held his neck down, threw his hood over his head, and listened to the knob twist as Collyn walked in.

"Bless!" She jumped. "I didn't know you were here." She flicked the lights on. "What happened?"

He stood up and walked over to her. "Come here," he said, hugging her. Her sweet scent filled his nose.

"Just tell me what the fuck it is. All that other shit can wait." He hesitated as he squeezed her tight. "It's not that great."

"Would you get to the point?" she said, aggravated.

Bless kissed her lips, "I just love you so fuckin' much." He buried his nose in the side of her neck. "So, so fuckin' much. You know, the day we met . . ." He pulled her back to him.

She knew he was stalling, "I don't wanna talk about the day we met."

"Just listen. Let me talk."

"Then talk."

"I just want you to understand that the way I feel and how much I love you wasn't a part of the initial plan."

"What plan?"

"I fell for you, but I didn't expect to. Which is what makes my love for you even stronger."

"Ooo-kay, do I look fuckin' impressed?" she asked, defensive. "What? You wanna step?" Her voice quaked. "Step—it makes me no never mind." Her throat ached, spitting out such a lie. "All I wanna know right now is about my business."

"I hate myself for having to do this." Bless placed his 9 mm pistol on the kitchen island and pulled his FBI badge from around his neck.

"What is that?" She blinked in disbelief.

"It's me—it's mine—it's who've I've been."

"And what is that?" Tears filled her eyes.

"An FBI agent."

"FBI?" She could barely say the letters without her throat closing up.

"I need you to understand that I really am in love with you and this didn't start out as an investigation on you."

"What?"

"I've been undercover for the past few months. We started out investigating Mayor Kenyatta Smith, but since he was dealing illegally with you, you just happened to get caught in the mix. I'm really fucked up behind this."

"Say that again?"

"I love you so much, Collyn."

"What?"

"Please tell me you believe me."

Silence.

"I've been going crazy. This shit is eating me up inside! Baby—" He walked over to her. "I need you in my life."

Collyn was dizzy. Her head hurt and her body ached. She could have sworn that Bless had said he was an FBI agent, sent to set her up . . . or somebody up. She could've sworn he'd said she'd been living an undercover operation for months. Did he say that he'd been lying? That their love was based on made-up shit? Maybe . . . maybe this was a practical joke, or an episode of *Hell Date* that had played out too long. Yeah, that was it. But then when she looked at him and saw the tears running from his eyes, the FBI badge, and the gun, she knew that this was real.

She rubbed her temples. This wasn't happening. Because he genuinely loved her, right? This was a dream, it had to be, because her breath was leaving and her feet were slipping from beneath her. She held her head up and looked at him. He had the same face and the same body of the very niggah who confessed his love yet spat on it at the same time. It was as if he'd opened her soul up and pissed in it. Her entire body burned and her mind raced.

So . . . he hadn't really been diggin' her when he said he was? And . . . he wasn't really in love? Or was he? Hell, was his name even Blessing Shields? How did she know that? How did she really know who this was standing in front of her?

Collyn squinted, bit down on her bottom lip, drew her hand back, and slapped the shit out of him. Bless stumbled, and before he could catch his balance, Collyn started swinging, punching, and screaming for dear life. She had nothing, and everything she'd thought she had wasn't even real.

"Collyn! Stop!" He grabbed her in a futile attempt to get her to calm down. It didn't work; she kept screaming, all the while swinging with everything she had. Then suddenly and without warning, she stopped. She simply stopped and looked at him. Her mouth watered and she bit her lip. She took a deep breath, dragged up all the saliva that she could from the heart of Jerusalem, snorted, and hog-skeeted it directly into his face. "Get the fuck out!"

The clock stopped. The air went stale. And the atmosphere silenced itself. Bless wiped his face and neck with the back of his hand. He stared at Collyn. The veins on the side of his neck thumped like an erratic heartbeat. He started walking across the room backward until he reached the front door, where he turned around and walked out.

Collyn stood shocked. Her entire life flashed before her. "Oh my God." She lost her breath. "Oh my God . . ." She leaned against her wall of windows and slid to the floor, while Bless sat on the opposite side of the door, his head tucked between his knees.

THIRTY-TWO

The cold breeze slipped through the cracked window in Bless' office as he sat at his desk, perfecting his game face. Looking at him, no one would think that he was dying inside. Three days had passed since his world had blown up. His routine had become mundane, trite, and he'd started to feel as if he did the same things all day every day: get up, go to work, and go home. It was hard to believe and even harder to swallow that they'd been to paradise and back, and now he had to ride through hell and deal with shit without Collyn. It was something he didn't know if he'd ever get used to.

Bless assisted the Missing Persons Squad with their case, giving them all the information that he had on Kenyatta. It was also the last day that Collyn would be able to accept the U.S. Attorney's offer for a plea deal, and Bless was on edge, worried whether or not Collyn would make the smart decision and turn herself in.

As Bless' thoughts carried him away and the heartbreak softened his chest, there was a knock on his door, causing him to look up.

"I just thought you would want to know that Collyn Bazemore and her attorney just came in. She's agreed to accept the deal," Agent Smiley said.

Bless rose from his chair.

"Conference room two," she said as she walked away.

• • •

Bless stepped into the room quietly, just as the other agents were explaining the plea deal to Collyn. He sat down in a chair and looked at Collyn, who quickly turned her head away from him.

Agent West slid the tape recorder toward Collyn. "Ms. Bazemore, I just need to inform you that this session is being taped. You understand that?"

"Yes."

"I just wanted to ask, what made you decide to come in today?"

Making a moment's worth of eye contact with Bless, she said, "I decided to come in because I'm pregnant."

• • •

It was midnight and Collyn had been crying for hours when the phone at her bedside rang. It was security. "Evening, Ms. Bazemore. Mr. Blessing Shields is downstairs to see you."

Collyn sat up on the edge of her bed, wiped her eyes, and sighed.

"Are you still there, Ms. Bazemore?"

"Yes . . . send him up."

When Collyn opened the door, they stood and stared at each other, each hoping and wishing they could simply forget the truth even existed and go back to the way it had been. But the hurt had already created a cold and hard distance, and Collyn spat, "What are you doing here?"

Bless' eyes roamed her body. Her red silk kimono hugged her curves. He pushed her hair behind her shoulders and their eyes made contact. She stepped back and he walked through the door. Collyn held the knob as she turned around, scared that if she walked too far away from the exit, she wouldn't be strong enough to ask him to leave. Pushing her heart back down in her chest, she said again, "What the fuck are you doing here?"

"You know why I'm here. I know we got fucked up in this shit, but you had to know that I loved you. You had to know that."

Tears danced in the back of her eyes as she felt her strong face fading and revealing her feelings. "You loving me doesn't mean shit. I've lost my business fucking with you. You knew I was going to be raided. That's why you insisted that we go to the Bahamas!"

"I swear to God I knew nothing about that!"

"You expect me to believe that?"

"I love you."

"Fuck you and that fucked-up-ass love! If you were there for Kenyatta, then you should've got with his ass, not me. And now I'm standing here, not knowing what the fuck tomorrow is going to bring, because for the first time in my life, I don't have a clue about what the fuck is really going on. Love me? You were investigating me! You ain't shit. As a matter a fact you're worse than any crooked-ass pig out there. You don't love me! The federal government paid you to fuck me . . . and you did. Satisfied?"

"It wasn't like that, Collyn. I know I hurt you."

"Exactly and I'm not gon' get over that shit! So if you're here about some baby"—she opened the front door—"then you need to leave, because after I left the FBI office this afternoon, that shit was a wrap."

"You didn't . . ."

Tears poured down her face. She hated that she was lying, but the truth was she didn't know what she wanted to do. She loved him and she wanted to have the baby, yet she couldn't imagine having a baby by someone she didn't even know. "Get out and don't come back!"

Bless walked over to her and grabbed her hand. She snatched it back. "Please leave."

Shaking his head, he hunched his shoulders and kissed her on the forehead. "I'm sorry, baby," he whispered. "I'm so, so sorry." He glanced at her one last time before leaving. After he was gone Collyn walked over to the kitchen island, put her head down, and screamed.

THIRTY-THREE

Kenyatta lay in the center of his king-sized bed, the back of his head making an indentation in the goose-down pillow while he stared at the vaulted ceiling. Thick clouds of smoke from the burning blunt, tucked in the corner of his mouth, did a serpent's dance into the air while Lennie Williams echoed in the background and rocked the historic bedroom.

He lay with a towel draped across his hard dick as he licked his fingertips and stroked his sex with warm saliva. Vibrations of the anticipated nut caused his toes to curl as he thought about the complete flip that his life had taken. No longer was Monday in bed with her knees tucked to her chest, wondering where he was and what he'd done. Now he lay waiting, masturbating and trying to figure out when the fuck did karma show up.

No longer was he considered a man of substance, one of high society, well respected, and with priority; ever since the City Council had asked him to step down, he sat at the center of everyone's attention because they wanted to impeach him. He was an embarrassment to America's greatest city, and not a day went by that there wasn't someone making sure he knew that.

Yet his greatest success to date was his ability to not give a fuck, and he would show their asses just how much. In two days was his state-of-the-city address, and he'd planned an elaborate speech in which he would address the city's budget and projected plans and then creatively tell everyone who didn't support him to kiss his ass. Fuck 'em, he didn't need 'em.

As the high of the weed started to have a nice effect and Kenyatta massaged his hard cock, his body trembled and his mind wished he had Monday's manicured nails scratching down his back. He missed her breathy voice whispering in his ear about the thickness of his dick, her hot breath running across the base of his neck. It wasn't that he didn't have any pussy to tear into and suck when he got ready, but it was other women that had ruined him, and now he needed to concentrate on becoming a family guy, which he could do if his wife allowed him to. And as far as her past, he had a solution for that. Somehow and someway they could deal with Collyn, since she'd been Monday's pimp, by setting her up, turning her in; making sure she went to prison. But had Monday answered any of his calls and given him the opportunity to tell her that? No, she was too busy enticing some niggah or so Kenyatta thought—to knock out the bottom of her pussy.

Kenyatta continued to play with his dick as he thought

about Monday sucking it. After a few shudders and chills, Kenyatta sat up, wiped his hands on the towel, and slid to the edge of the bed.

He took the blunt dangling loosely from his lips and blew a stream of smoke into the room. He couldn't remember when he'd last settled for being treated like this. He looked at the phone and thought about whom he could call for advice, but since he'd been caught up in so many scandals, so many people were turning their backs on him that he didn't know whom to trust.

He thought about how this was about much more than losing a marriage, being unappreciated, and being emotionally damaged. That was the easy shit. But this . . . this was a whole other level of violated commitment that other people's mortgages, kids, bills, dogs, and shit couldn't even fuck wit'. Your average everyday heartbreak had nothing on this. This was about upholding an image, maintaining power, prestige, and position. This was about him not being able to step away from the walls of City Hall. And he needed his wife to stand by him while he proved to the haters that without a shadow of a doubt he wasn't the niggah they needed to fuck wit'.

Tired of being fucked up behind shit he couldn't change at least at the moment, Kenyatta lay back down and drifted off to sleep.

• • •

Hours later he heard the door creak. "Monday?" Kenyatta opened his eyes to see her standing at the closet packing her things.

"Oh, you just gon' come here after being gone all this time and pack clothes like it's nothing? Where have you been?"

Silence.

"I asked you a question."

Monday sighed. "This whole nightmare is over with. This marriage is over."

"What the fuck do you mean it's over?" He shook his head and a muscle on the side of his jaw twitched.

"What part of that don't you understand? I am just tired of all this shit!" As she spoke she threw clothes into her suitcase. "You fuckin' anything that moves! Having babies and shit all over the place. Misappropriating funds! Missing bitches or should I say dead ones. And then you rolling up in here like you can beat my ass any damn day of the week. I'm tired!" she screamed. "This ho is going on the stroll. I'm the fuck out. You worthless piece of shit! You're nothin', Kenyatta, nothin', and I'll be even less if I stay with yo' ass!"

Kenyatta stood still and his eyes narrowed on her, "This sounds like some niggah been up in your head."

"Yeah, and everything else too! Now get the fuck out my face!"

"What? I'll kill you before I let you leave! I promise you that shit. I will kill your ass! So you better tell that niggah to get on! You sick of me? You knew who the fuck I was before we came up in this piece. You know I love you, and now you wanna act like it's nothing, Geneva."

Monday looked in his face and laughed. "Love? All the times I cried, laid up here, and wondered where the fuck you been. And each and every time you were out with some bitch, telling her a buncha bullshit. Love." She laughed again. "You don't even know what love is." She resumed packing her clothes. "Selfish motherfucker."

"I said you ain't goin' nowhere!" He pulled his hand back and slapped her, sending her flying across the room. He walked over and slapped her again. Monday's eyes widened and she swung her arms as if she were doing the backstroke. She squirmed on the floor. "Get off of me!"

"I'm not gon' let you and some niggah ruin me! You need to tell whatever niggah it is to get ghost because I'm not lettin' you go that easy. 'Cause we in this till death do us part!" He tossed her across the room, causing her to fall into the night-stand and topple everything over. As she scooted back, banging her head against the wall, she spotted her gun, which had fallen from the nightstand to the floor.

"I don't fuckin' believe this shit!" Kenyatta spat. "After everything I've been through, this is what you do? This is what the fuck you do? You ain't shit, bitch. That's exactly why I was fucking around. You can't expect no man to be faithful to no ho."

Monday felt as if horses stampeded through her mind as she reached for the gun.

"And even dead," he went on, "Eve is more of a woman than you'll ever be!"

As he turned to slam his elbow into her face, Monday pointed the gun toward him. "You better back the fuck up!" she shrieked, tears and sweat pouring down her face. She could feel blood dripping from the corner of her lip. Her head felt as if she'd been beaten with a bat.

"What you gon' do?" he sneered with a smirk on his face, looking at her with disdain. "Huh?" He hunched his shoulders. "What?" His mind flashed back to the day he was fucking Eve and she was shot dead. His eyes roamed all over Monday's bruised and battered body, and he knew that at this moment she was capable of anything. "So is that what you did, bitch, when you shot Eve in the head?" Kenyatta walked closer to Monday.

"You better back yo' ass up!" she snorted. "And get the fuck out!"

"What you gon' do, Monday, shoot me?" He continued to walk toward her.

She knocked the safety off and he stopped dead in his tracks. "I will kill you." She didn't flinch, and although tears blinded her eyes, she had a clear aim of where she would burn the bullet through his chest. "Now, you can die or you can leave peacefully, but either way you gettin' the fuck outta here."

"You gon' shoot me, Monday?"

"If I need to. Now you talking too motherfuckin' much. And I only have one word to say: goodbye."

"This the motherfuckin' mayor's mansion. How the hell you gon' put me out?"

"I mean it."

Not able to gauge if she would really shoot him or not, Kenyatta grabbed his clothes from the floor and backed out of the room slowly. "Ai'ight, ai'ight, I see what the fuck is going on here."

Monday stood still, unmoving, with tears pouring from her eyes. She didn't know what to do, so she stood with the gun pointed at the door and didn't relax until she heard the car pull out of the driveway. Then she completely fell apart.

THIRTY-FOUR

In the shadows of the New York City skyline Kenyatta was in his secret Central Park West apartment, haunted by paranoia. His mind continued to replay the night Eve was killed here as he searched each room, the wooden floor creaking beneath his feet. He scanned through the closets, and followed the dim trails of light drifting in from the windows to every crevice of the apartment. Beads of sweat ran down his face and over his eyes.

He paced the room and then walked over to the bar and poured himself a double shot of Vodka.

Unable to calm his nerves he picked up the phone and called Hudson, "I need you." He said as she answered. "Right now."

"I'm on my way," Hudson said without hesitation. "Where are you?"

"I'm not at the mansion. I'm at the 4114 Central Park West apartment—" Before he could finish she'd hung up.

Kenyatta held the phone in his hand for a moment and then he placed it on the hook. He walked back over to the bar and took steady sips of vodka to the head. His chest burned and his mind raced as he rose from the bar stool and began to pace again.

He took another shot of vodka and heard a knock at the door. He opened it and Hudson was standing there. He pulled her inside by her arm, and once she was in the apartment, he stuck his head out the door, looked both ways behind her, and slapped the three deadbolts on.

"What's going on?" she said in a panic.

"I swear to God . . . I swear . . ." Kenyatta paced, the sound of his voice rattling with a drunken tremor, "This shit is crazy."

"What? What's crazy?"

Kenyatta let out a deep breath and paced a few seconds more. He knew he had to resolve this . . . he had too much to lose not to. The problem was he couldn't wrap his mind around what he needed to do. He needed things to get back to the way they were, but no one ever told him how to rewind time.

"Damn," he said, exasperated. If only they could just get through this, he would never cheat again; obviously anything that tore up his life and career like this wasn't worth it. Which is why he'd called Hudson. She was, among other things, his personal advisor, his chief of staff, and certainly she understood more than anyone else how he desperately had to make this shit work. Otherwise his political career was finished. "Hudson," he cupped her chin, "you're the only one I can talk to."

She gave him a look of assurance, "Yes . . . I am."

"Which is why I'm going to tell you this." He started pacing again. His mouth was hesitant to spit out what his mind insisted had to be true.

"Kenyatta," Hudson grabbed his hand, "I'm here, what more do I need to do to prove that to you? I don't wanna be in the closet anymore. I want the world to know that I love you."

Kenyatta stopped dead in his tracks and spat out as if he'd never heard a word Hudson said, "I think . . . I think . . . my wife killed Eve."

"What?" Hudson blinked, frozen in her spot. "You think Monday did what?"

"Everything just happened so fast. She must've snapped. She must've thought that these bitches out here meant something to me. She didn't have to do this. Didn't she see we were a team, that I needed her to run this city?"

Tears surged from Hudson's eyes. "What does that have to do with killing Eve?"

"Maybe—" He clinched his fist, "Fuck! Why did she do this? She didn't have to, she could've talked to me."

"She doesn't love you. She doesn't appreciate you. It's me. I love you. I appreciate you."

Kenyatta continued, oblivious to anything Hudson was saying. "And you know what?" He wiped his brow, "I fucked up. I really, really fucked up. I should've just told her the truth."

"Do you even know the truth—"

"Eve was stalking me."

"Stalking you?" Hudson took a step back, "You haven't heard a word I said, have you?"

"Eve wanted all of my attention and I knew Monday was jealous. She must've found out about this place somehow, broken in here," he turned around toward the hall closet and pointed to the missing door, "and lost it."

"Since you think Monday killed Eve, why don't you call the police?"

"The police? On my wife? Are you fuckin' insane? Let me tell you something, that's my fuckin' wife. Not my jump-off, not my baby's mama, not some ho'n-ass bitch in the street, but my wife. Be clear. Yeah, we fight, and I say shit to her, somethings I mean and some shit I don't mean. But so fuckin' what? Do you know how many bitches in the street I say I love you to? But at the end of the day, fuck them. I know Monday may have done some shit—"

"You said she was a murderess!"

"She did it because she loved me."

"She doesn't love you! I love you!"

"How the fuck did this turn in to being about you?"

"We are a family—we have a baby—"

"What the fuck?" Kenyatta spat, as if it just registered where Hudson's head was at. "We're not a damn family. You knew my situation, you knew I had a wife who I was never leaving. You knew exactly what this was. A good fuck and nut suck. And be clear, we had a baby, because you didn't use anything, no other reason. Don't get it twisted."

"I don't believe this."

"Believe it. Your job is to help me maintain my power and position politically and all that other shit is extra."

Hudson stood stunned, doing her all to hide the fact that she was visibly shaken. She didn't want to cuss and scream, because that wouldn't solve anything and sometimes the best words were left unspoken. She swallowed and stroked Kenyatta's hand. "You're right, Kenyatta, I was out of line. Forgive me."

"You're too selfish sometimes, Hudson. You overdo shit. I'm

going through something right now and I need you to understand that."

"I do and you will rise above this. You always defeat adver-
sity. Now what did you do with the body?"

"Tracy helped. I told him not to tell me what he did with
the body. I didn't wanna know."

"Smart move."

"This has me fucked up. How am I supposed to give my
speech in the morning?"

"You will give your speech. And you will do fine."

"I never expected shit to be like this."

"I know, but you need to recognize who you are. You are
Kenyatta Smith, the mayor. You are the one in charge. This is
your city and no one can run you out of anywhere. So I need
you to be strong, because we are going to rise above this. You
have the love of the people. Everyone knows your heart. They
have nothing on you and nothing to tie you to her murder. As
a matter of fact, if that body is not found, no one can tie you
to anything."

Kenyatta looked at Hudson. "You think? You really think
so?"

"Yes." She stroked his crotch. "I do. Now let me make you
feel better." She unzipped his pants and slid his hard member
into her wet and warm mouth while Kenyatta placed his hand
on her shoulders and tossed his head back.

THIRTY-FIVE

Kenyatta was escorted by his security team to the stage where the state-of-the-city address was to take place. He looked into the sea of flashing lights, reporters, cameras, and invited guests. It didn't matter that none of the City Council took their expected and assigned seats behind him. He was here because obviously this is where he was supposed to be, regardless of what was really going on around him.

Kenyatta stepped up to the podium, tugged a little at his silk burgundy tie, hunched his shoulders, and began his speech. "I come humbly before you," Kenyatta's round gold-frame glasses rested on the bridge of his nose, "as not only the mayor of our great city but also as a man, a caring man, a kind, an honest man, who loves this wonderful place."

Out of habit Kenyatta turned to his right where Monday usually would stand and reach to grab his hand, but instead of her being there, he spotted Hudson standing at a distance in Monday's spot. She smiled at him and he turned back around.

"I come before you most humbly and most honored to be your mayor," he continued. "We have made great strides together, and since I have been in office, we have been like a family. Despite all the things that the lynch mob media wants to blame on me. We, New York," he spoke with the confidence of a great preacher, "have been together, supporting one another, and for that I thank you. Going forward we will continue to focus on decreasing the city's deficit, cracking down on prostitution rings that seem to be sweeping our city, bringing down crime, drug dealers, guns, the murder rate, gangs, address the homeless situation, and together we will stand and together we will continue to build a great city." Once the notes containing his speech were done, Kenyatta continued on. "No longer will I be plagued by the political mob run amok who disrespect me and lie on me about foolery of which I have nothing to do with. I am dedicated to this city. I stand strong, and City Council," Kenyatta looked at Thomas, "we have more important things to take care of in our city than for you to entertain nonsense. So, as I bring my address to a close, I say thank you, New York, for supporting me and allowing me to take us to a better place. I bid you farewell."

Kenyatta nodded his head and was escorted backstage by his security. "Bless," Kenyatta shook his hand and nodded his head, "it's been a minute."

"Yeah, it has been," Bless cleared his throat, "but look, can you step over here for a moment?" Bless pointed to a remote corner of the hallway.

"Sure," Kenyatta said with certainty.

"After you." Bless held his hand out and Kenyatta walked in front of him. Once they were standing in the space Bless had designated, he looked at Kenyatta and said, "Please place your hands behind your back." Before Kenyatta could protest, Bless took his arms, placed him in position, and slapped handcuffs on him.

Kenyatta tried to snatch away, "What are you doing?" he said, noticing an army of FBI agents standing around him. "Nice to see you again Mr. Humble," Agent West said as he nodded his head at Kenyatta and Agent Jones waved.

"Bless," Kenyatta looked confused, "what the hell is going on?"

"Mayor Kenyatta Smith," Bless said, "I'm Special Agent Shields and you're under arrest for obstruction of justice, misconduct in office, perjury, money laundering, and the murder of Eve Johnson."

"Murder!" Kenyatta screamed, "I didn't kill Eve!"

"You have the right to remain silent," Bless continued on, "anything you say can and will be used against you in a court of law."

Kenyatta heard Bless, but his mind wasn't there. His memory tripped through all the times he should've known better than to trust anyone other than himself, and by the time he came back to reality he was in the back of a federal agent's car, with the sirens blaring and a television camera stuck in his face.

THIRTY-SIX

The afternoon sun crept into Collyn's room as she lay in the center of her bed, wondering where all the black had come from. She knew it was noon, because the digital clock said so, but all she could see was space. Space everywhere. No longer did she see an exquisite Manhattan penthouse with amenities fit for a queen. All she could see were empty rooms with haunting echoes that wouldn't let go of the sound of his voice, the memories, the essence of his touch, and his fuckin' scent.

Collyn wanted to scream and cuss out the world, because nobody, not her mother, her father, or her cousin Taryn, had ever told her it would feel like this. Everyone had always said, "When a man hurts you, to hell with 'im." But never had they mentioned what to do about your heart wanting him back.

She stared at the cathedral ceiling and thought about how her life was so different now. Everything was different except the way she felt about Bless. She loved him. She knew what he'd done to her was fucked up, but no matter what, and despite all of that, she couldn't stop the craving she had to hear him laugh, see him smile, or hear him tell some corny-ass joke.

She missed the way he would call her and just tell her he loved her, he missed her, and he simply wanted to hear her voice. She wanted to hold his hand again and just be by his side. After all, they did share a life . . . But then again, fuck him.

Collyn shook her head. If only the memories would just leave.

She got off the bed and walked into the kitchen. She pulled the carrots out of the refrigerator and placed them on the counter, grabbed a knife, and started chopping them for her garden salad.

Doing her all to distract her mind from thinking, she started to sing. Eventually she found herself singing at the top of her lungs, only to have tears sneak into her eyes and pour down her cheeks. She looked around the empty room, and before she knew anything she was screaming and screaming and screaming until all she could do was rest her head in the crook of her arm and cry until her tears made a river on the countertop.

THIRTY-SEVEN

Monday stood on the balcony of her hotel suite and looked at the busy Manhattan street. She wondered where her life would go from here. Was she actually welcoming independence, or was it loneliness? She knew she wanted to rejoice that she'd finally left Kenyatta, but the pain rocking the center of her chest needed soothing. Yet she couldn't go back to him. Leaving him wasn't about no longer loving him; rather, it'd become a choice of life or death. And she had to live, otherwise she would never know if anything would ever be different. She had no choice but to face her greatest fear: being alone.

And yeah, she had regrets. But this was life, and sometimes that was just how the shit went. Despite the many nights she'd spent praying for him, somewhere in the midst of it she'd always known it would all come down to this.

She walked back in the hotel room, and turned on the TV. She flipped the channel to ABC News where the commentator announced "Mayor Kenyatta Smith has just been arrested."

FIVE MONTHS LATER

THIRTY-EIGHT

Bless sat with his head thrown back and his hands in the side pockets of his pants. It was eight o'clock in the evening and he was at the local bar, knowing that it'd been five months too long for him to still be in mourning. Mourning his heart aching at even the softest breeze that carried Collyn's scent. At the thumping of car tires in the rain that reminded him of how she would jump when they splashed water on the curbs. He couldn't stand to see her favorite TV show or listen to her favorite song on the radio. Every time he smelled the scent of her perfume he choked up. And he couldn't stop thinking about how she drooled in her sleep.

He hated that they didn't meet under different circumstances, because maybe then, they would've had a million chances to get things right. But they didn't and here he sat listening to Earth, Wind & Fire on the jukebox preach about the reasons for love.

"Deep thought?" a tall and curvy woman walked up and slid onto the stool next to Bless.

He sat up and looked into her face. She was pretty, long eye lashes, about a size ten, attractive enough to command some attention. He smiled at her and she returned the gesture. He could tell that she was diggin' him. No matter the anguish he felt inside, on the outside he was still sensually brown and beautiful. "Yeah," he said, his deep voice radiating with sadness, "I was thinking. It's cool, though. How are you?"

"I'm fine." She blushed, and immediately his mind flashed back to the first time he met Collyn. As he fought off his memory he heard her say, "I'm Tina, and you?"

It took a few moments for him to answer; Earth, Wind & Fire's preaching was so intense that Bless had to contain himself and remember that it was a song and not a sermon. He noticed Tina trying to get his attention. She waved her hand, "Did you hear me?"

"Nah," he cleared his throat, "my fault, what'd you say?"

She smiled, "I asked your name."

"Bless . . . Blessing, as a matter of fact."

"What a powerful name." She looked him over as the bartender stopped in front of her and asked what she was drinking. "Amaretto sour please."

After receiving her drink, she pressed the glass to her lips, took a sip, and then proceeded to talk to Bless. He was doing his best to listen, but the music seemed to be speaking directly to him, and he wanted to hear what Philip Bailey had to say, after all he seemed to be going through the same things.

As Bless listened, he wondered where Collyn was, what she was doing, where she was going, and who she was with. The tips of his fingers could still feel her soft skin pressed against his, causing him to shudder at the memory of what she felt like.

Bless knew he was fucked up, but he needed a way to get out of feeling like this. For the longest he'd sat in front of the building where Collyn lived or across the street from her gallery, waiting for the right moment for it all to click and he would be able to walk away peacefully.

Which is why he was here at the bar, because he figured . . . fuck it . . . and fuck her. He could drink a couple of beers and somehow learn to live without her. Hell, if nothing else, he had pride. And besides, she wasn't the only one who was hurt. What about him? He confessed everything to her. Told her all that she needed to know. Risked his career, his life, and everything that he worked hard for to save her. And what about the jokes he told her, the times he called her and told her he loved her? What about how he would massage her feet and make love to her like the world was coming to an end . . . and still she didn't appreciate him. What about the Chinese food, how he took care of her when she was sick, and was right there whenever she needed him . . . and still none of that was good enough. So to hell with it then. What choice did he have other than to pack his emotional bags and keep it movin'.

"So are you single?" Tina interrupted his thoughts, "You look like a nice man, I'd like to call you sometime."

Bless saw her lips move, but he didn't respond. How could he? He'd just convinced himself of some bullshit he knew didn't exist, and at that moment he knew he couldn't go another day without seeing the only woman he ever wanted in his life. He had to try, at least one more time, and if it didn't work, then fuck it. Fuck . . . it . . .

THIRTY-NINE

Collyn's face glowed in the summer sun as she spoke to the customers walking around her art gallery. She laughed as Taryn told her a story about what her daughter had done in day care the other day.

Collyn's life, with the exception of the painful regret that danced on her heart, had completely changed. She no longer ran her family business. Red Light Special had come to an end, and now she was into simple shit: HGTV, Chinese food, and the local news. She'd even put her apartment up for sale and started looking at houses in Jersey, which she hoped would be someplace she could escape to and pretend that the loneliness she felt every night before going to sleep didn't exist.

A customer walked over to her and asked, "Hey, Collyn, can I place my order with you now?"

"Of course."

She took the order and glanced up with a smile as she handed the customer his receipt and he walked away. Suddenly her heart raced in her chest and her bottom lip trembled. She swallowed and nervously stroked the sides of her hair as she looked directly into Bless' face. They locked eyes for a moment, his expression telling her that he knew he was taking a chance being here.

"Beautiful," he said, "I tried, and it didn't work out for me." Bless spoke as if he were exhausted.

Collyn remained silent, doing her best to hold the tears in the back of her eyes at bay.

"I promised myself that I wasn't going to bother you. You know, I figured you hated me, that I was shit to you. And I know I deserve that, and that's why I bounced, but every day I thought about you. Every waking hour. I wanted to smell you, make love to you, hold you and never let you go. And every day I try to let you go and say, 'This is the day that I'ma get over you.' It never happens, and the next thing I know I'm making the same promise to myself all over again.

"I knew I was taking a chance coming here, but I waited long enough and I had to say something. At least try one more time."

Although the gallery was filled with people, all Collyn could see was Bless' face as his words soared through her heart.

Collyn walked from behind the counter, and Bless' eyes immediately locked on her six-months-pregnant belly. "You kept the baby," he said in disbelief as they moved toward each other.

"Listen." She cleared her throat, remembering where she was, "Now is not a good time."

"Well, when is a good time?" he asked. "Because I need to talk to you."

"That may be true, but you have to give me some time. I will call you."

"I'm not leaving. Ain't nothing for me to wait. You had a better chance of me leaving before you came out from behind that counter."

Collyn sighed and looked at Taryn, who signaled with her hand that she could call the police on his crazy ass. Collyn shook her head and said to Bless, "Come with me to my office, please." She turned back to Taryn and held her index finger up as a signal that she needed a moment.

Once they reached her office and she closed the door behind them, she said, "What do you want?"

"I want you."

"You can't have me."

"But I already do. You gon' tell me you don't still love me?" He moved in closer to her.

As she went to move out of the way, he stepped into her path. "Look at me. If you look at me and tell me to bounce, I'm out. I'm done. We'll make arrangements for the baby because I'm not leaving my child, but I won't bother you if that's what you want. But I won't stop loving you, because I can't. I tried and the shit won't go away."

Collyn wanted to tell him to leave, but she couldn't get the words to fall from her mouth. Tears fell from her eyes as he walked up close to her, her protruding belly rubbing against his body. "It doesn't have to be like this. Just give me a chance." He placed his lips against hers. "Give me a chance." He took the back of his thumb and wiped her tears away.

"Why is everything with you so urgent? I need some time to think." Collyn took a step back.

"Let me tell you something," Bless said. "Me loving you *is* urgent. Me needing you back in my life is an emergency. I need you right the fuck now and I ain't walking away without you."

"But Bless—how am I supposed to get over this hurt?" Her voice cracked.

"By letting me love you." He walked up to her and whispered while looking into her eyes. "I swear I will never lie to you again. I put that on my life. But I love you and yeah, maybe right now I'm being pushy, and selfish, and a pain in the ass— but I need you to understand that I love you and it ain't shit more urgent than that."

"How are we supposed to do this? Where do we begin?"

"Right here." They began to kiss passionately. "We begin right here."

FORTY

The sun crept into the sky, and the first light of dawn shone over Mehki's and Monday's brown bodies as they moved in tune with each other.

Their lovemaking was sweet, soft, and easy, and they moved in a sensual dance with each other, their bodies making promises that they would see each other again, but their minds knowing that this had to end.

Monday gasped as her body quaked beneath his, rocking to their own rhythm. While Najee played softly on the clock radio as they bathed in heat and dripped with the physical evidence of their passion, their screams echoed through the apartment, intensifying the orgasmic gifts they were leaving with each other.

Monday lay her head against Mehki's chest as her mind tripped over the many memories she had. Her life as Monday Smith was no more. It was time for her to redefine who she was, which was why she wasn't moving. She was staying in New York to face the music. She'd taken the bar, passed it, and had accepted an offer at a criminal law firm. She didn't know what awaited her, but that was the chance she was willing to take.

"If you ever decide to come back to me, I'll be waiting for you with open arms."

Smiling, Monday said, "Who knows, maybe one day I just might run into those arms."

FORTY-ONE

Hudson stared at the aged and smeared Plexiglass that held a ghostly remanence of fingerprints from everyone who'd journeyed through here. The buzzing and constant chatter of people around them provided a melodic version of the new level their love had reached. She saw Kenyatta going to jail as a way for a renewed opportunity. A way to put a halt to him loving Monday and perhaps pay her more attention; especially since all he'd heard from Monday was that she was divorcing him.

The plan for Hudson was to stick by him, help him beat the charges, take the baby, and they would ride off into the sunset.

Ever since she dropped the anonymous tip to the FBI about Tracy Robinson and he quickly turned state's evidence, along with Collyn's testimony Kenyatta was right where Hudson wanted him. In an orange jumpsuit, a black-painted number across his left pec, a turned-up palm pressed against the bulletproof plastic, and a chipped black-painted phone receiver held to his ear.

"I gotta get the fuck outta here," he spat at Hudson with a glimmer of tears in his eyes. He banged his head against the plastic, "I swear to you I didn't kill this bitch!"

"I know you didn't," she said sorrowfully, pressing her palm against his, "because I know you, and I know what type of man you are."

"Then get me out of here!"

"I'm trying, but they won't give you bail."

"GODDAMN!" he screamed, banging his fist on the table in front of him; the correction officers gave him a warning eye as they moved closer to where he was.

"Calm down, baby." She looked at the officers and gave them a reassuring smile. "We don't want to alarm anyone."

"Have you found me another attorney, since Mehki's ass quit? Dumb motherfucker."

"All of your assets are frozen, and the best I was able to do was get you a public defender."

"Public defender? What, are you trying to keep me in prison?"

"No, baby—"

"Don't baby me—you don't give a fuck about me. Monday would've never done no shit like this. She loved me. She was ride or die for me. What good are you? You're useless. And I'm sick of your bullshit. Now, you get me a real attorney."

Hudson stared at Kenyatta, refusing to let a single tear slip from her eyes. Here she was again. With him spitting vicious venom, never acknowledging how much she tried and how much she had to deal with. Didn't he know how much she loved him or was this the part where she figured out that love didn't have shit to do with this? "You never loved me, did you?" she asked him.

"Hudson," Kenyatta said, attempting to calm down, "do you know what I'm looking at here? Along with all the other shit, I have a murder pinned on me that I didn't commit."

"I have done nothing but try and be good to you."

"Now is not the time for this."

"And I watched you as you looked at Eve, like you loved her. A look you never gave me."

"What . . . are you . . . talking about?"

"And you fucked her over the sink, just like you did me that night. You stroked her with passion and fire, and I watched you desire her while I sat in the shadows crying."

"What are you saying?"

"I cried when I found out you had a secret spot that you took her. I cried and cried and you never cared. All you thought about was you. I followed you there a thousand times, and the night I was able to get in I couldn't take it any longer. And I had to do it. I had to."

Kenyatta stood up and started banging on the Plexiglas as if he would be able to get to Hudson. "You killed her!" he screamed. "You bitch! You killed her!"

"It was the only way I could get through to you . . . but what did you do?" Hudson spoke mechanically, almost as if she were remote controlled, "You used me and you played me. And so I say touché." She stood up from the hard metal chair and straightened her skirt out, smoothing the wrinkles with the back of her hand. Kenyatta continued to scream as she let her end of the receiver dangle off the hook. She placed her purse on her shoulder, lit a cigarette, and left Kenyatta standing there screaming.

ABOUT THE AUTHOR

RISQUÉ is the erotic pseudonym of an *Essence* best-selling author. *The Sweetest Taboo* was her first work of urban erotica. She lives in New Jersey where she is working on her next novel. Visit her online at www.myspace.com/risquetheauthor.